The Time Traveller

VINAYAKA MOORTHI

WORDIT ART FUND

This book has been fully funded by the Wordit Art Fund. Wordit Art Fund
helps deserving authors publish their work by providing monetary
support. To apply for funding, please visit us at
www.BecomeShakespeare.com

First published in 2017 by

Becomeshakespeare.com
Wordit Content Design & Editing Services Pvt Ltd
Unit - 26, Building A-1, Nr Wadala RTO, Wadala (East),
Mumbai 400037, India
T:+91 8080226699

©
ISBN: 978-93-86487-03-2

DEDICATION

For Michel de Nostredame who carried time in his chalice.

ACKNOWLEDGMENTS

Thanks to the ways I happened to travel, for taking me right here. Thanks to the errors happened, for the outcome became faultless.

आत्मैव कर्मणः पूर्व-
मन्यत् किम्चिन्न विद्यते
ततः स्वेनैव कर्माणि
क्रियन्ते निजमायया॥

(दर्शनमाला : श्री नारायण गुरुदेवन्)

CONTENTS

Before the story begins

This is a story that links two centuries together with an unfulfilled love; its zest brings back a life from one era to the other. It reincarnates the long lost dreams of two human beings.

One man who lives in Coventry, United Kingdom in the year 2014 travels not only across the English Channel to a Serbian Village, but across the barriers of time to the life of Serbia in 1914 leaving his own world. It might sound impossible for us, but we never know the secrets of this universe. We never know how this world was created nor do we have a detailed knowledge on when it was created.

Time is just a matter of perception that has been followed. Everything is trapped in a pre-planned flow of time, days, nights and stars; even us. Are we sure that we are truly real? Are we really sure that we really live here? Can we assure ourselves that today really exists? It could all be a dream, someone's dream in a mild sleep. Or it could be a dream that we dream ourselves somewhere far away. What we believe as our life could be just a dream that is dramatically seen. We

8

might wake up into a normal life after this dream. We might wake up into our real life realising that what we called 'death' was actually an awakening.

So let me tell you this story when this young man happened to travel across the barriers of time, back into the history of our world, behind our own shadows, to some lives hundred years back.

This accidental travel to 1914 makes Nick's life dreadful as his memories and knowledge clearly mirror a century ahead. He is unable to remember anyone from 1914 but he remembers his wife Andria who lives a century ahead in 2014. He is looking forward to meeting Andria again by travelling hundred years ahead. But without knowing the way forward he is stuck in Serbia in the beginning of twentieth century.

What happened in 1914?

1914, Village of Barič, Serbia

Lisie and Doruf, they were sitting on the banks of Sava River. They were unaware of the political traumas growling at their lives as they didn't do any mistake or hurt anyone. Why would they worry about an attack if there were no enemies for them? Lisie loved Doruf and Doruf didn't just love but devoted her. She was everything for him. Even when there were rumours around the entire Europe about a possible war between each nation for power, he was least concerned about it. While most of the men across Europe began to chant their national anthems and their heroic history, Doruf simply worked on his farm, adored Lisie and wrote poems about her smile in secret. They simply loved each other. They thought that was enough in their life.

As time elapsed in that fine evening Lisie hurried to get back to her home before the night wind starts to blow from the north. She tried to push Doruf from her lap.

'Doruf, let's go back. It's going to snow'.

'Oh, can't we sit a little more?'

Lisie normally agreed to Doruf's ideas, she liked the way he delighted her. She liked how he rested in her lap in every evenings and how he let her feel safe. She didn't disagree with him, instead she pointed what concerned her,

'What if it snows Doruf?'

'It won't take too much to reach our home; I'll give you my wool'.

'And you?'

'That's fine, cold doesn't bother me much, and you know that'.

'How long are we going to be here?' Lisie gently moved her fingers through his hair. Doruf had her left hand held close to his face admiring their engagement ring.

'We no longer remain lovers after this Sunday', he said that with a smile on his face. He glanced up to see her reaction.

'We will be, we won't change. Be the same Doruf'.

He leaned forward and cupped her face in an attempt to kiss her lips. They exchanged their love for each other beside the Sava River and slowly the sun began to hide behind the woods. Their houses were very close to each other, they were from the same village that spread from the Sava River to the end of the corn farms. There were very few residents in their village; they never met with a famine because what they made in their soil was more than enough for all of them. Light brown corn fields looked endless with a few shacks among them like canoes in a still lake. The light wind touched the grey leaves making them dance like waves in the lake. It was their village, their soil, where they were born to enjoy the immense beauty of life. Their young lives had a great way ahead to live in joy; they believed so like all happy ones. Destiny looked and looked at them and didn't take its eyes off when they started heading back to their village.

But before they even crossed the marshes to the cornfields, they heard a loud explosion. When they opened their eyes they could see a very dark mass of smoke rising above their village. They stared at it, they were safe. She pulled him back, unwilling to go anywhere near the explosion. But then thoughts of her parents and family who were trapped back there dampened her of all her fear. She stumbled after him.

The same loud explosion happened again and again and it ceased to stop. They fell on their knees as they couldn't stand up against the fury of the detonating bombs. It shook their feet off the ground and held them down. As the shattering rounds came to halt they recovered their senses and looked around squinting hard to locate the unusual sound, now audible; it was from a machine, a war machine. They took their hands off their ears and opened their tightly closed eyes. Smoke covered the entire sky and the fading sunlight failed to outreach the black smoke over their village. Their village had already sunk into the darkness before light bid farewell to the day. There was nothing left for them except the rounds of machine gun fires, flames and wretched screams.

Something they were least concerned while being busy loving each other consumed everything they had as their own. War, it started like plague. It was the beginning of a war that lasted for years. Their innocent blood was shed marking a milestone in the history of political hypocrisy. Lisie and Doruf, they were a little away from their village still they were in the range of gunfire. Lovers were always unarmed; there was no difference in their case too. They had nothing else to do rather than hiding wherever they could. Doruf struggled to find a perfect place for them. He wanted a tiny place where he could at least hide Lisie from the ravaging military troops.

'They're coming, they're coming this way'.

Lisie didn't know what to say, she just looked at the forwarding army. They were firing everything alive, even cattle and the village dogs.

'Come, Lisie...run'

Doruf pulled her hand to snap out of the shock. They ran away from there, using the maple trees as a cover and shielding their head with their bare hands. They thought it would be enough to outrun the bullets. Their thought didn't last long indeed.

'Lisie....'

He dropped her hands for the first time. Pain from the bullet would have been so severe; otherwise he would have never done that. He pressed the left side of his chest while calling out her name. It didn't take too long for his creamy white shirt to turn red. He fell down before Lisie's eyes. Lisie almost fainted seeing his blood dripping on the dried leaves. Doruf managed to say one more word,

'Run'.

Lisie sat down holding his hands and his blood spread on her skirt. His voice was inaudible but his eyes told her to run for her life. Her tears dropped one after one into his open wound and melted in his blood.

'Don't leave me, Doruf. I am afraid, I am afraid. Don't leave me alone'.

Doruf wasn't able to say a word, he was out of breath. The advancing armed men surrounded Lisie on their gun point. Lisie uttered one last sentence before they dragged her from Doruf,

'Doruf, don't leave me.'

'I can't lose you Lisie, I want to live', he was trying to say that but his lungs had no air left.

   Those were the last words Doruf heard and that was the last sight he saw before the absolute darkness rushed into his eyes. He died.

History is Seldom Remembered

History is like an empty shell that became pale white in the course of time, having lost with each molecule of moisture in the summer sands. What we know about the past are skeletons of some lives, reality is often forgotten; the flesh and blood.

What happened with Lisie after Doruf's death is unknown thereafter. But that day marked the beginning of another war in the history of mankind without any doubt. It continued for years rumbling towards the world, changing the world's face forever. History remembered their village and the day it was sacked by the heavily armed force; the empty shell. But their love, story and blood rotted in the mud; the reality. Lisie's warning about the snowfall came true, there was a snowfall that night. It erased the stain of blood when the moon slowly passed across their corn fields.

Doruf's dead body perhaps was among the others which were graved together beneath ten feet of soil near the river. Lisie's fate would be different as she was beautiful. She was very fair with a little bit of sun tan as she worked in the mustard farms nearby. She had long and curly hair that resembled the colour of the setting sun and her lips were small. Her fingers and neck were fairly long, even at her twenty three she looked like a beautiful Austrian teen girl. How many more women might have vanished from the world during those years leaving no trace and how many more men would have given up their lives like Doruf? It is certain, they all had one last hope before they closed their eyes for the last time; life with their loved ones, at least for some days. But they have nothing different from the story of Lisie and Doruf, the same forgotten lives. Lisie's beauty would have made her death very slow and painful.

The war ended and the world moved on with the survivors to another war. From there the world again moved on in the terrible memories of the past as days continued to elapse slowly consuming the lives to its shadows. Months passed with the changing seasons and then months became years and years became decades and the world changed, so did the lives in it. The faster life became the smaller the world turned as travelling across the world became less challenging. Everything was possible with the speed of the new world, but there was one thing that remained impossible, 'travelling across time'. No one travelled back into their life, no one travelled to the future neither did any back into the past. The days passed were always counted with the memories as one among the other lost days.

Whatever happens in our lives we always forget them, whether it is terrible or joyous we continue to live on. Lisie went into the mystery but 1914 and Doruf walked into the past giving way to the new moments, new days and years.

The world reached 2014 without both of them, a hundred years ahead.

A new home

Kenilworth, Coventry, England, 2014

'I'll get the delivery, it must be the sofa', Nick walked to the door with a cup of coffee in his hand as if he had been expecting someone for a long time. Andria, his wife was busy arranging their kitchen, newly bought plates, oven, electric mixer and many other groceries covered up their whole place. They just moved into the outskirts of Coventry city from London saying goodbye to the rush metro life. Nick wanted to stay somewhere very silent with fresh country air, and he had been thinking about it for the last seven years soon after he sensed the loneliness of being in the crowd. Surrounded by strangers all the time, a group of men and women unwilling to smile at each other, neglecting the beauty of each morning while rushing after the so called rat race of living; London was never his home. Kenilworth seemed perfect for him, a little away from Coventry city, a place with not much traffic or pollution, a place where people smiled at each other and found delight in knowing each other. But the very reason of preferring Coventry was

Andria, she was from Coventry and it was there they first met.

Nick's intuition was correct; it was the van from IKEA* with a mushy comfortable sofa. But the sofa was placed in its place only after Andria was done with arranging their kitchen and all other rooms. Finally they made it possible, a house of their own. They laid leisurely on their new sofa drinking some wine.

'Rose wine! Oh please, not again?'

'You know I love it, don't worry I have some beer left for you', Andria gave him a can of beer.

'A big day for us, isn't it Ann?'

'Yeah, it took a little long though', she continued, 'But we made it, nice country air, a little garden, enough rooms and a car porch. This is exactly what we wished'.

'Yeah, fair money. Not too expensive.'

'Yes, it's truly perfect'.

Andria rested her back to the sofa and with a long exhalation she stretched her spine. Nick gently pressed her back and massaged her shoulders. He could see it in her actions that she was absolutely tired. He came up with an idea as he wanted to relieve her from the works of the night.

'Ann there's a restaurant at the corner, you must have seen it. Let's go out explore our new home. Don't cook. It's too much elbow grease for today'

'Wonderful, it'll be good. I'm in no shape to cook'

'Perfect, go get ready then it's just a drive away'

There wasn't much delay; they drove their blue Ford to the Punjabi restaurant at the end of their street. The restaurant was a little crowded like all the other Indian restaurants, especially with the Indian students. They spotted some European men and women as well exploring the exotic spicy food and stuffed Punjabi sweets. They claimed the reputation for alerting all the taste buds in human mouth. Andria liked food, especially Chinese and Indian. She always preferred those when they go out for a change. There were times when Nick made fun of her saying he would buy an Indian sari for her when she regularly ate Indian meals. And one day when Andria was into spending some money on cloths his fun backfired at him. Inspired from his regular teasing she decided to get a very fine Sari that was made in India. It shined with its sparkling design and stone works, but Andria soon realised it wasn't that easy to wear a Sari, and it was only after a week when she tried it on the occasion of her friend's birthday party. It took her half an hour to complete it even with the help of her Indian friend Neena. Andria had different choices and tastes, she wanted to try everything possible, dress, food or culture. She was always open to the wide world. Nick chose that Punjabi restaurant to make her happy. He made sure each time he appreciated her tastes. And that night they had a wonderful dinner from there.

They were a little late after the dinner. But still Nick wasn't done with the day; he wanted to buy some beer to celebrate their first day in their new house.

'Where will you get it, it's too late. We'll have to go to TESCO* for that'

'It's not far from here, they've a TESCO* close to the City Centre, they're running twenty four seven', Nick said.

'Alright that sounds determined.'

'Let's go get them. We should drink tonight, or when?'

Nick searched Ann's face for her agreement. Andria nodded saying,

'Okay, beer is going to be fine. Don't even smell them when you drive'.

'Okay, Honey, that's a deal'

Their Ford went a little wild with Nick's intentional push on the accelerator.

'Nick, keep him slow'.

It seemed Ann succeeded in bringing down the gear with her scream. Their car slowly headed to the nearest TESCO* in the city.

IKEA : A shop, mainly for home appliances

TESCO : A supermarket

First morning at Kenilworth

March 12, Wednesday, 2014

The beauty of most houses at Kenilworth was their wide glass windows opening to the garden. Nick's new house was similar; it had a wide glass window. Flowers in their small garden smiled at them carrying the morning mist over their petals. It was a wonderful morning to wake up to the day. Andria was sober, but their first day in their first house was rising with a fine morning while they slept half naked. A responsible wife like Andria didn't take too much to think about a bed coffee for her husband. She turned around towards him and kissed his cheeks before leaving the bed. Nick was in a deep sleep he didn't even feel her kiss. He was perhaps enjoying a nice dream. But certainly that dream took him far away from Andria making him powerless to feel her. It took less than ten minutes for the coffee to reach him.

'Good morning Nick, wake up time. Coffee, coffee'.

Andria placed the coffee on the table beside their bed. Nick's sleeping pill bottle was lying beside his cell phone on the table. He had to use them for the last few days as he didn't get enough sleep. It was prescribed for him by his doctor.

'You can call sick if you want, it was tough, yesterday. You've got enough sick leaves, don't you Nick?' Andria continued while picking up the empty beer cans and glasses. There were some nuts scattered around their bed, they were all the remains of their beer night.

'I think we should get a nice table lamp for our room',

Andria was getting annoyed with his sleep; she turned around to his face.

'Nick, your coffee is getting cold. Wake up'

Nick didn't even respond to her voice as if he was sedated.

'I'm going to burn your toes with the coffee cup, wake up', she awaited him at least to move away from her but nothing happened.

'I'm coming for you, she said.

She touched his toe fingers with the coffee cup very quickly expecting he would jump from the bed, still nothing happened. She put the cup again on the same spot and kept it for a while till he shakes it off, but nothing happened. Andria began to sense danger. She put the coffee on the table and grabbed his hands and shoulders trying to pull him from the bed. She called him many times to wake up. She called him again and again. She broke into tears, but she managed not to break down. She put her ears on his bare chest and heard his heart beats. Tears flowed through her cheeks while she was calling his name, she struggled to breath. His heart was beating, he was alive but he didn't wake up from his sleep. She couldn't even pull him from the bed to her lap as he was of no balance at all. She ran to their telephone and dialled the help line number.

Before they arrived with help, she was trying her best to wake him up. Her calls didn't wake him neither her tears.

'Relax madam, relax. He's going to be fine. Let me see'.

They positioned his arms back and forth repeatedly and rubbed his feet and palms. But he responded to nothing and remained unconscious.

In the eyes of Andria and others he was unconscious but he had already opened his eyes in a different world. But nobody could see it. He was conscious about his existence and what was happening. He was searching for Andria, his love, in a strange place where snowfall was a little too heavy. He was with Andria still in a sense as she could still touch his unconscious body but where was his consciousness? Where was his mind? The doctors didn't know that neither did his Ann. He was carried to the hospital in an ambulance within no time. But he was awake; he was somewhere else away from everything he knew; away from everything he was partially obsessed with. He felt completely secluded in that new place. He walked along those hazy village roads in the middle of a vast cornfield. He could see some shacks far away with dim lights and many cattle sheds. He hurried towards them, he was scared. He didn't know where he was, he didn't know how he reached this bizarre place?

A mystic travel

Somewhere in time

Fear is fear because of little familiarity. He walked along the path free handed heading towards the light, leaving behind fresh corn buds in each step. He was afraid because he didn't know where he was. Life took him on a journey without his permission to a new shore, strange and vast to the horizons. Every man on earth has been the same, all of them might have travelled through different places in their lifetime, places where they never wanted to be, places they never dreamt. But life goes on unveiling more secrets each moment that come across. The path of our life is uncertain, but if thought well, it is this very uncertainty that enlivens hopes in our lives. Uncertainty is the ploughed fields and hopes are the seeds of life to be scattered.

He was walking under a heavy snowfall in that strange place in the night. He knew he was not supposed to walk over those lonely roads especially while it was heavily snowing. But there was nothing he could do about it. His thoughts were all revolving around one question in his mind, 'Where was he?'

His weak body couldn't stand against the heavy snow that directly shot to his chest. His legs started to freeze to the roads. He began to fear that he wouldn't be able to walk to the wooden houses those were right in front of his eyes. Those hamlets were still a little far away from him, he felt like his legs were stuck in a marshland. He struggled to lift each step from the road as if his feet were glued to the ground. Churlish gravity, he began to sense an exceeding weight on his shoulder that slowly spread to his entire body pushing him down to fall flattened over the white thick snow bed. The tall corn plants stood solemn around him. The snow kept falling over his body and cheeks, frostiness sacked his hands, neck and his pale fingernails. His eyes were slowly closing, he was fainting. As he closed his eyes he was aware that it was a dream, he could see Andria and some hospital staff in their light green uniform walking around him, they were hurrying in an attempt to save his life. He could see Andria. He understood that she was crying, he wanted to tell her that he was alright. He wanted to tell her that he was safe, but just lost somewhere in his hallucinations for some time.

He knew he drank too much beer in the night and took two sleeping pills right before going to bed. He was intelligent enough to argue for himself that he was just high with the drinks he had but he was absolutely wrong. He was suffering from a stroke. He tried to touch Andria's face to wipe out tears from her cheek but he couldn't move his hands, he tried again to move his fingers but they didn't obey his will. His vision began to fade away. He could see that wild winter night and the cornfields of which he dreamt. It was right behind Andria. The hospital room slowly disappeared along with Andria. Everything was fading into the cornfields very slowly like the moon fading behind the clouds. The hospital room, the hospital employees in their green uniform and the bright electric lamps in the hospital, everything faded away from his eyes. He was dripping himself like drops of honey, smooth and thin like a line into a new time where Andria didn't exist, neither the hospital, his new house or in a sense himself. Time barriers flipped in him, when he opened his eyes he couldn't see anything that was familiar, nothing belonged to him in that completely unfamiliar rural roads. He lost everything, his wife, his world and even his own body in a matter of just a few seconds.

He was lying in the snow wearing a light cotton shirt but he wasn't freezing, he stood up and shook off the snow from his body. His eyes were gazed to the hamlets right before him. They were sleeping in the dim light of electric lamps when he was born again. They didn't know he was born again. He didn't know that he was born once again in that place.

Eyes opened to absolute strangeness

Village of Barič, Serbia, 1914

Looking around to the wild winter in his attempt to figure out the place certainly didn't work out well. What men know about this universe is nothing, what we know about our own lives are the same. Otherwise why would our minds weep when meeting with a strange new path in our own voyages? We are like the sparrows in the cornfields, making little nests among the thick leaves hatching our off springs; learning from the days that pass giving ourselves bit by bit. And when we learn enough from one angle we move on to one different place for a fresh beginning. It is how this cycle rolls on.

He had to step forward; there was no step back in this game of uncertainty. His throat was dry like a piece of brick; it was yearning for some drops of water. Looking everywhere in the light of the moon for a stream or a lake in vain he kneeled down as if he was struck down by lightning. He picked up a handful of snow from the road that was already covered up with a thick layer that reached above his ankles. He chewed it in his mouth for one or two seconds and swallowed the few drops that melted out. His thirst was soothed at least for a while. That boosted him to walk towards the lights. Until reaching to the lights his feet kept moving even though they were frozen; they turned pale like a pair of white wax feet.

He knocked the door of the first house from the cornfields, one that stood a few steps up from the level of the road. It was Murfine's house; he lived there with his three daughters and wife. It took a few minutes for Murfine to open the door; he was probably scared. There was an uncertainty prevailing there all around the European continent about the political relations between each nation, especially between Serbia and Austria. No one was sure what would happen in the next day, it was absolutely unpredictable. Bari was near the border of Serbia, their cornfields ended at one point at a fence. Beyond that fence the soil was the same as it was best for corn and mustard and sparrows were same as they made their nests among the corn leaves. But it wasn't same in the eyes of men as it was called Austro-Hungary. It was the soil of Austro-Hungary; whatever grew there was Austrian whether it was plants, animals, men or perhaps even the wind.

'Who is there?' there was a silence for a while. Murfine was anxious; he carried a long rod of iron that he used in his farms for his own safety. He asked again from behind the door in the native Hungarian language,

'Who's out there?'

'I'm Nick, I am..... lost... here. I... don't know.... this place, I'm so.... cold. I need..... some fire.' Nick wasn't able to talk, he uttered the sentence in many broken words. He didn't understand Murfine's questions. But they continued to speak in their own languages. Murfine knew some English, he understood intentions of Nick but he was not ready to allow anyone in his house.

'Just leave, don't play with me. Get away from here'

'Please, I have no place to go. I don't know this place'

Murfine heard Nick falling down in front of his door on the wooden floor. Murfine slowly began to change his mind, his anger and insecurity began to fade away. He knew this trespasser was a foreigner from the way Nick talked. His English was absolutely in the tone of a native English speaker. Murfine was basically a kind hearted man. He knew it was his duty to give this stranger a shelter in that freezing night.

'It's too late in the night to travel through the ways you aren't sure about?'

'I know sir, but I don't know how I reached here. Don't know who took me here'

'What? You mean you're kidnapped?'

'No sir, I don't know. Nobody kidnapped me. I can hardly talk, I'm freezing here'.

'How can I trust you?', Murfine wasn't ready to open the

door for a stranger. He had three little daughters to take care. There wasn't any reason to question his weak hospitality.

'I beg you sir, just for a while. A little bit of fire to warm my skin'

'I'm going to open. Are you English? You sound English'

'I'm, I'm a British'

The door was opened for him but Murfine was carrying the rod in his hand till he saw Nick very close. Nick walked into their sitting room where the fire was still hot enough for the house. He showed his hands to the fire and stretched his legs too. Everyone in the house looked at him in wonder as if they couldn't believe their eyes. They looked at each other in disbelief. Murfine's daughters ran towards their father and hid themselves behind him. Nick wasn't surprised to see their reactions. Everyone would feel the same if a stranger walks into their house in the middle of a night. Nick tried to smile at them but as they all stood speechless he turned his face to the fireplace. Without looking at their faces he thanked Murfine,

'Thank you, thank you for letting me in'

Murfine walked towards him very slowly, but the girls stood away from him. Murfine touched his shoulder and asked him in Hungarian,

'What happened to you?'

Nick didn't understand him, he politely said that he didn't

know their language. He said,

'I'm sorry, I don't understand your language. I'm new to this place. Where is this?'

Murfine looked at his wife's face with disbelief; he didn't know what was going on. His wife walked a little closer to Nick. Murfine looked at him and wiped off the remains of snow and water from his body. Murfine asked him in English,

'What happened to you Doruf? Why did you walk in the night?'

'I'm sorry sir, my name is Nick. Nick'

'Get up, just relax, you see who this is? You see Jane?', he pointed his fingers to his younger daughter. She looked at him and tried to smile but she was too scared to smile.

'No, no, sir. I'm new here, I don't know any. I don't'

'Don't you remember me, my name, I'm Murf'

Nick didn't understand what was going on. But he felt something strange when everyone looked at him as if they all knew him before. Nick wanted to cry because he was confused to the depth of his heart. He asked himself,

'What happened to me, oh God, what happened to me?'

Nick turned his face to Murfine and said,

'I don't know you, I don't remember any of you. Where am

I? Where am I?

Saying that Nick burst into tears, he cried like a lost child. Before Murfine could hold him he fainted and fell over on the wooden floor.

First step to the parallel reality

Village of Barič, Serbia, 1914

'Ann, come closer. Don't hide behind those shadows. They are between us trying to pull us away'

There were a few villagers in Murfine's house when Nick was whispering in his sleep. But, Nick wasn't Nick anymore; he was Doruf even though he didn't believe it. That was one way to look at this situation; the way the people around him saw and believed. They thought their friend Doruf went out of his mind and act like an English man called Nick. They declared that Doruf is mentally ill.

There was another way to look at this, the way Nick thought about himself. He believed he was right, he said he was Nick. He thought only he can be right. The base of every trouble in the world is the same as we all believe that only our ideology can be true. We hardly ever travel through both ways and explore both sides. Nature gave two eyes, two ears and two hands to explore everything twice, from both sides. Nick was lucky, perhaps the chosen one to reincarnate into the times of Doruf to see things from both sides to tell us about the secrets of time. But Nick was still being the Nick who didn't believe in Doruf. He wasn't ready to accept Doruf who lived within himself a hundred years before he became Nick. It is the instincts of mankind, perhaps a curse upon us that we seldom remember our history.

The people around him were all either his relatives or friends or at least they all knew him very well as Doruf but the problem was he didn't know Doruf. The whole room was filled up with whispers and eyes of disbelief.

'Did he say that? He doesn't remember us?'

'Mmm, he said'

'He had gone mad I think'

'Don't say that, he is a nice man'

'Does she know yet? Lis?'

'No, Lisie will die if she sees this'

'That is so true'

Conversations about him carried on inside Murfine's house until Doruf's father Vincent arrived there. He was a local medic. He had travelled around Europe several times just to satisfy his thirst to travel in his younger days. He had seen situations more critical in his lifetime many times. So he wasn't shattered seeing his son in somebody's home freezing and uttering senseless words. He told everyone to move aside to give enough air for his son. He didn't try to wake him up, he just checked his eyes and covered Doruf's body with one more layer of wool.

'Murf, heat up the room a little more. He should sleep. I think he was just sleepwalking'.

'That's okay, let him sleep here'. Murfine hesitated to say what he was about to say. Vincent understood he had something to say, he asked him,

'What are you hiding Murf, what do you want to say?'

'That's..'

'Be frank, let me know what it is'

'He wasn't sleep walking for sure, he had his eyes opened. He was talking in English, like an English man. He didn't understand when I talked in Hungarian. He said he don't know Hungarian'

'Oh, lord Jesus.'

'We were worried to see him speak that way. Jane was terrified, she still is. You know how close they are. It was a little too much for Jane'

'A sleep would make it better, let's hope', Vincent was optimistic as a medic should always be. That was his speciality. He continued to Murfine,

'If he's not well tomorrow, we will get him to a psychiatrist'.

The village was too small for a secret to remain secret. It reached to the other end of their village and the news became a lot more than reality as it travelled a long way. At Lisie's house the news reached flavoured not just with a tinge of modification but with a ruthless conversion. The news was taken that far within such a short time by Veronica. She told Lisie that Doruf will never be her Doruf again. She woke her up from her sleep and said,

'Lisie, Doruf is gone mad. He became mad, he forgot everyone. He's at Murfine's house, the whole village is there. Who knows whether he will be alright ever?'

'No'

Lisie felt a severe pain inside her ribs hearing Veronica. She had her engagement ring on her finger. Veronica looked at it with her cold blooded eyes like a wolf staring at a lonely lamb. Veronica was envious of everyone who enjoyed love and every husband and wife in the village ever since she became a widow after a few months of married life. She never went to any wedding; she never went to see an engagement thereafter but always attended every funeral in their village. She said that she must be there to send them back from the world. Veronica was sad hearing Doruf but her twenty seven years old envy became happy seeing the end of a possible marriage.

'Go, see him, I should get home now', Veronica began to leave saying that. Lisie knew that she wasn't going home, she knew that she was going to spread this news everywhere. Lisie stopped her and scolded her, it was for the first time in her life she became wild. She didn't even know what she told Veronica. She said,

'You're not going beyond the border to Ausrtia to sing it, or will you? Will you?'

She didn't stop, she couldn't. That is something strange about love, it makes everyone blind when it is their own call. It gives courage, pleasure, freedom and jealousy beyond our imagination. It even intoxicates the blood in our veins with hatred at times, no matter how innocent you are. We hate, avenge, betray and sacrifice only for love, what makes the difference is how we love? We hate someone when our love for ourselves is questioned, we take revenge for our loved ones. We might betray someone for the sake of our love for ourselves. Sometimes men even sacrifice their own lives for their love for somebody. It is love that makes the base of every other feeling. Thus it is just a matter of one question, how we love?

Lisie shouted at her like a hound,

'He will be alright, you hear me? You bitch. Sing this everywhere you go but you'll not see us separate. I'll even die for him, I'll even die. You don't know that, do you? Dying for love will be impossible for you. Go away from here or you'll see your grave tonight. I'll send you to the dead'

No one expected Lisie to be that violent not even her own parents. It was for the first time in Veronica's life she was absolutely frightened with the words of another human being. Veronica couldn't go anywhere else to spread the rumour; she was petrified in the volcano of love. Lisie rode her horse through the snowy road, no one could see her tears as they were shaken off from her cheeks with each step her horse took.

Lisie and Doruf? Or Lisie and Nick?

Lisie and Doruf and their love, the whole village knew how much they cherished each other and everyone knew they would marry soon. But Lisie made one enemy in that snowing night, a deadly enemy who pledged herself to destroy the lives of anyone once they stood in her way. It was Veronica's mission to abort Lisie's marriage from the moment she raised her voice against Veronica. Feeble sound of the wind swirling through the wide cornfield and lonely trees that stood among them heard Veronica talking to her heart.

'Lisie will never marry Doruf, I won't let them stay together'

It was Veronica's love for herself that sparked her hatred to Lisie; it is from the fountain of love everything begins, even hatred. She shouldn't have loved herself so much to hate another. She should have learnt to balance it to forgive her own fate and to change her own fate in the long run. But, time rolls and things keep happening as it is meant to happen. This cycle has to roll over the universe.

Lisie reached Murfine's house almost at the same time Veronica reached her own house. When Lisie sat on the bed near her Doruf without knowing he was Nick Veronica dragged a chair towards her over the wooden floor and sat alone thinking about the ways of tearing them apart. Veronica couldn't take in the feeling of being questioned by a young girl. She couldn't forget the words Lisie fired at her pride. Lisie hugged her dearly loved Doruf very gently without disturbing his sleep and held her cheeks on his chest for a few seconds while a little away from them Veronica was grabbing tight on her pillow releasing her anger towards Lisie. That roll of cotton twisted between Veronica's fingers.

'Take me back to my Ann, Ann', Lisie couldn't believe what Doruf was whispering, she took her face back from his body like she was completely shaken with an electric shock. She looked at his face a few times checking whether he was awake. Her eyes were already filled with tears hearing her Doruf whispering about some other girl. She tried to hear everything he was whispering about; she kept her ears close to his lips.

'It's not my place, it's not my place. I don't want to be here', he continued saying things. He was complaining about his worries in a dream.

'Not my people', he said.

'Ann, where are you? I don't see you. It is too late, too cold and snowing. I am lost.'

Lisie put her face away from him to not to disturb his sleep with the tears that dripped from the corner of her eyes. She wiped her tears very quickly and listened closely to hear if he said something about her. She couldn't believe that her fiancé, her own Dorf had another woman in his life. Lisie held back her sobs within her heart and heard what he said.

'A lonely place, cornfields around me, I'm so cold. God, show me my Ann', He was weeping in his sleep.

'I'll find you Ann, I'm coming for you'

Lisie wanted to run back to her house, to her room and cry out all her pain that consumed her. But she didn't want anyone to know what Doruf was talking about so she kept everything inside and wept laying her face on the same bed in all silence. Nobody was in the room to disturb both of them so he kept whispering and she kept grieving over her loss. She couldn't keep her sobs inside for a long time, she had to release them. That was enough for him to wake up, he woke up into the parallel reality of Lisie and her love. He saw her lying beside him and weeping, even though he didn't understand her at all, he could understand from the way she wept beside him that those tears were meant for him. He tried to move pulling his body with his weak hands.

'No, no, please stay on the bed. You're very weak', Lisie told him in Hungarian. He didn't understand what she told but with her actions he understood what she meant. He said in shattering voice in the language he knew, in English,

'I'm Okay lady. I'm feeling better'

Lisie looked at him in bewilderment, even though she knew

43

English she didn't understand why he talked in English. She didn't understand why he called her 'lady'. She didn't want to confuse him with questions, so she didn't bother about clarifying him.

'Dorf, just sleep, you look tired. I'll sit here till the morning, I'm with you', she kept on talking in Hungarian. She leaned over to his face to kiss his lips, but he gently pushed her face aside.

'What are you doing, girl?', he asked

Lisie couldn't believe her eyes, she was bleeding inside. But she hid everything for Doruf. She asked him in Hungarian,

'Why do you speak in English?'

He looked at her having no idea about what was she talking about. Waiting for his reply in vain Lisie used English,

'You are talking in English, why?'

'Because I'm English, I know only English. I've no idea about your language'

'Do you know where we are?', Lisie was sensing something strange in her Doruf. Veronica's words echoed in her ears, 'Lisie, Doruf is gone mad. He became mad, he forgot everyone'.

'No, I don't know this place. No'

'Do you know who I'm?', Lisie was afraid to ask that question, a fear grew in her eyes while awaiting his reply. Her fear came true, he told her,

'No, I don't know you'

Lisie sat speechless. She put both her hands against her face and sat without uttering a single word looking right into his eyes. She felt that the whole world was going through a great invincible silence and she began to feel that she had lost her life all at once.

Nick gets to know Lisie

Nick was feeling better, he wasn't feeling cold and the room was heated up a little more when Vincent instructed Murf, but still the identity of Doruf was unknown to Nick. He began to grow a suspicion in his mind about Doruf; he asked himself several times why they called him Doruf and why they behaved as if he was very familiar to them. He couldn't satisfy himself with an answer. He simply was helpless in his new world knowing nothing about it like a new born. He looked at Lisie's face who sat beside him looking straight into his eyes without even blinking her beautiful pair of eyes. He could see it on her face that she wasn't comfortable with the situation; it was the same for him. He wanted to ask her many questions as she was alone in the room. He wanted to know what actually happened to him, how he reached there and more importantly who actually was Doruf.

'Hey, I don't understand what's going on here?', Nick started to talk with her.

'I am trying to figure out where I am, I don't even know where it is. Is it Coventry or some other city? Let me tell you this, I am perfectly alright. I am just lost in your village.

46

Believe me, lady'

Lisie kept looking at him, she wasn't able to believe her eyes nor her ears. Everything seemed absurd to her like others who were waiting outside the room. But she didn't want to push him into more confusion. She thought it would be nice to let him talk whatever he wants to say. She gave him head nods in support as if she wanted him to talk. She gave him the expression that she understood his problems. She was ready to do anything to get him back.

'Which city, you were saying? Coven..?', Lisie asked him.

'Coventry, you don't know Coventry?'

'No, I don't know it', she wasn't very fluent with her English but she talked with him very easily.

'Oh, okay. So which is this place, which city is this?'

'It's not a city, this is a village, Bari . Do you know Bari ?

'No, I don't. Which part of Britain is this? I have never heard about Bari .'

'Britain? You mean English land?'

'Yeah, England. The UK.'

She looked at him, she was puzzled whether to say it to him that it was not anywhere near Britain. She didn't know what would be his reaction. She wasn't sure how far Britain exactly was, she tried to remember the world map. Germany and France then the sea, England was far away even to have a serious thought about it. But she was ready to mention it. She wanted to know how he would take it.

'This is not England, not the UK. It is away'

Nick looked into her eyes very deep seeking the answer for his question. He was sure the answer was somewhere hidden in her eyes.

'Where am I, where are we?'

'Serbia, we are in Europe.

'What?', he couldn't believe his ears. He checked whether he heard something else.

'Did you just say that we are in Serbia, this is Serbia?'

'Yeah, we are'

'Impossible', he said and looked around the room and outside to see something familiar. It was snowing outside; he was absolutely shaken to hear where he was. He asked her,

'How, my passport, how did I travel? I didn't fly, didn't sail, then how?'

'Did you come with someone else?', Lisie talked to him as if she was able to understand his position.

'No, I was alone. May be not, I don't remember anything about coming here'.

'I slept last night I remember, just there with my wife. She was with me, it was our new house. We were a little drunk as well. I don't remember coming here. We didn't even have a plan about travelling to Serbia'.

When he said he had a wife, Lisie was burning inside. But still she talked with him,

'You might have just forgotten things. Sometimes people loose memory, you know. But I am sure she is somewhere here looking for you. We'll find her in the morning'

'Could it be so? Is she going to be safe here?'

'She'll be', Lisie looked down and she hid her engagement ring with a pillow that lay beside him. Without showing her worries she asked him,

'What's your wife's name?'

'Ann, Andria'

'You call her Ann?'

'Mmm...mmm', Nick murmured in acceptance but he was totally confused. He was still thinking how he reached Serbia. He was forced to agree to Lisie's idea that it would just be a memory loss, they might have travelled together. 'She must be here, it might be just my memory trouble, I can't remember anything about it'.

'May be a sleep would bring back your memory, sleep well'.

'Yeah, may be', he thought the same. He thought with a sleep he would be able to recollect where Andria was and how he travelled to Serbia. But Lisie was expecting the other extreme; she hoped he would wake up in the morning with her memories, which meant without the memories of Andria.

'Eat something if you are hungry, it will give nice sleep'.

'No, I am not hungry. Thank you for helping me'

She smiled at him and put his pillows close. Nick noticed her engagement ring. He asked her,

'Your name?'

'Lisie, I'm Lisie', she told him as if she didn't even know him. But it was hard for her to hold her tears in her eyes while acting like a total stranger.

'Your husband?', he asked her about her husband without knowing he was actually her fiancé. She was shocked for a moment without knowing what to tell him, but she said without much delay,

'Oh, he, he is at home. He is sleeping. I think he is very tired', she was shaking while saying it.

Lisie asked him like a total stranger,

'I forgot your name, you are?'

'Nick'

'Oh, yes Nick. Good night then Nick'

'May be you can just stay in the room for a while, it feels

strange here, but when you are around I feel calm. I'm a little scared to be here alone'.

'No problem. Don't worry, I'll be here till you wake up'.

'Thank you, Lisie. Good night', he closed his eyes while Lisie said,

'Good night', she said very silently,

'Good night Doruf', he didn't hear her. He slept very well trusting her.

Strange path

Night went away silently shivering in the falling snow and presented a fine morning to the village on her way. Morning sun fell over Nick's face before Lisie woke up, she was sleeping sitting near the cot resting her head over the bed very close to his face. When he woke up to the new morning in his strange place, he saw her. She was gorgeous; her hair fell off of her forehead covering her face a little bit. He gazed at her trying to remember about the night that just passed, trying to remember about meeting this beautiful young girl.

'Lisie', he reminded himself without waking her up.

He tried to remember how he reached there. He was able to remember everything, falling snow, lonely roads in the middle of the cornfield, dull moon light, knocking at the door of a strange man's house, meeting Lisie in the night, asking her to stay in his room as he was afraid to be alone in the new room, hearing from her that he was in Serbia, but how he reached there still remained unexplainable. He stretched his hands to touch her to wake her up, he felt he could trust her for a reason still mysterious. He didn't know he once lived the same life she lived, he didn't know he travelled back to the past and met his own love in the past. Lisie or anyone in Serbia didn't know or could imagine that he came from future; a hundred years ahead of their time, their present time.

Our life if we say is a magic of light, we call a ball of light that gives energy from trillions of miles away from us Sun we say it is trillions of light years from us. When our planet turns, half of our people call our own shadow as nights while the other half calls the light as days, we make mornings out of this light, we make evenings out of light and when the night sky is clear we see the reflection of light on the moon that is far away from our eyes and we love calling it the moon forgetting it is sunlight that makes the moon bright. As earth revolves around the sun this game of shadow goes on telling us a lie that one day has passed, telling us another lie that another day has begun and these lies make our life. So what actually is our life? Is it a lie or an illusion of the sun light? We never know, we think we live we think we will die when our time comes and take a new form perhaps. But do we really do that. Light is a magician that gives us a feeling that we are living, creating fake days and nights and by doing so giving us a feeling that years have passed and months and weeks. But in fact nothing happens, time is just a feeling. Time doesn't exist at all. Time is the very mysterious but interesting work of magic from an immensely talented magician, the light.

Some people say they can foresee future because they are close to the creator God. Some say it is possible if you are gifted with the ability of bending light to foresee the future. So when I say the story of Nick, don't get confused with Doruf. How Nick left Britain, how he travelled with his memories and attached himself in another body. Once you are totally fallen into the orbit of light, it can take you to places where you were, may be one day ahead, may be one day in reverse or sometimes far away from the century you believe you belong because for the light it is all the same whether it is today or a million centuries away; in the regime of light the concept of time doesn't exist. It was there from the beginning, it is there and it will be there forever.

'Lisie', he called her.

Lisie woke up quickly and looked at his face, she couldn't hide it that she was waiting for that call. She held his hands and asked him,

'Yes, tell me. Are you okay now?'

She had only one thing to ask to the Gods, to give his memory back.

'I'm feeling good. I feel thirsty, could you give me some...'

Even before he finished the sentence her hands picked up the jug that was on the table, she poured water into a glass in a hurry and gave it to him. She looked at him watchfully while he drank from the glass.

'Lisie, I should find Ann, my wife'

Lisie's face turned pale with hopelessness, she understood that he still wasn't able to remember her. But she had to tell him something, she had to ensure he could talk freely with a person who will not treat him as a mad man. So she pulled herself to act the role of a stranger with perfection. She told him,

'Yes, I remember that. But I've to tell my family before coming with you and you have to eat your breakfast before we go in search of your wife'.

'We can have something from the shops, please tell your family that it is very urgent. She must be worried. We can complain to the police'.

'Okay, but there aren't any shops here, this is a village'.

He had to accept her words, even though he was hungry he just wanted to go. Lisie brought him something to eat. After finishing breakfast Lisie gave him a jacket to wear. Even though it wasn't snowing it was still cold.

'I've to tell you something'

He looked at Lisie's face with curiosity. He thought she was going to tell him how he reached here and where Andria was, there was nothing else in his mind.

'What is it?'

'Everyone will talk to you in our language. Don't talk to them in English. Just smile at them, pretend that you are still weak and always be with me. Don't go anywhere without me'

Nick couldn't understand what was happening. He looked at her with his eyebrows wrinkled.

'Why would I do that? What's wrong?'

'Okay, I will tell you. Listen carefully and stay calm and patient. It might sound unbelievable but you have to trust me'

'Tell me, I believe you', he was curious to know everything.

'You look very much alike one of us. You look like Doruf. Doruf doesn't speak English like you, he knows it but he's got a different accent. Trust me, even I am not able to believe you are Nick'

Lisie introduced him to himself; she began to tell him about Doruf. Nick was being slowly exposed to the life of Doruf and Serbia.

'Doruf is a farmer here and he is engaged to a local girl. His father is outside this room. He is Mr.Vincent, I will show you. It'd be nice if you smile at him pretending that you know him very well. Just act like you are sick and if he asks you to go with him. Tell him you are coming with me. Use gestures to talk with everyone, just pretend that you are really weak to talk'

Whatever Lisie told him to do, he agreed to everything even in his disbelief. He said,

'Well, take me out to the police station. That's all I want'.

But Vincent wasn't outside the room luckily so Nick didn't have to take more strain to act as Doruf. He did everything he could to make others believe that he wasn't well enough.

But as he was leaving the living room of Murfine's house, he noticed the newspaper on the table. It looked very old to him without any pictures on it. He took the newspaper in his hand, it wasn't English. But on the top of the paper beside the news paper's name something grabbed his attention. It wasn't any news because he couldn't read that language; it was the date of the paper. It was written, 'June 17, 1914'.

A terrible reality

'Lisie, could you read this news for me', he showed the newspaper. He looked still as he had lost all his mind, Lisie understood that he was terrified but she didn't understand what made him to tremble so much in the newspaper.

'Why, what's wrong?'

'Please read it for me, the first main news'.

'Okay, I'll', she read the news and tried to translate it to him in English.

'Peace of Europe foresees a major threat; Russian army strengthens its armoury'

'Lisie, the date on the newspaper'

'June 17', she looked at him without any idea about his thoughts. He couldn't wait, he was getting annoyed. He tried not to show his anger, but it was in his tone.

'The full date, Lisie the full date'

'Relax, I'm reading. June 17, 1914', she couldn't hold her tears. She looked at him in tears. She couldn't understand what happened to him. She asked him trying to hide her sobs,

'What's the matter, what happened to you?'

He stood there, he wasn't able to look at her face. He looked up to the clouds; he wanted to yell at his fate. He felt helpless when he came to know about the time gap between his existence and the place where he was standing with Lisie. He understood he had travelled not just a long way far out to the country sides of Serbia but through the concept of time. He knew he is supposed to be in Coventry, England and live in the twenty first century in 2014. But however he wasn't there, he wasn't even in the time he belonged. He touched himself, touched his own hands and cheeks to make sure of his existence he pulled back the jacket from his hands and saw his hands. There was something unusual about his body, he could see a different skin. He was sure he was alive, he still wanted to breathe, if he was in land of dead it wouldn't be the case he guessed. But that even wasn't certain, the dead might need air they might even need to breath. He had no proof to assure his mind that the dead didn't bother about breathing. He was reminded of a tattoo over his right shoulder, he did it before he married Andria in 2005. It was just one letter inside a heart, 'A'. He was very young. He forgot he was standing at the door of Murfine's house; he started to take his jacket off and unpinned the buttons of his shirt.

'What are you doing?', Lisie asked him in disbelief. She

wasn't sure what he was about to do, she tried to stop him.

'Stop it Doruf, stop it', She was silenced with his look, she paused as if she was reminded about something. She called him 'Doruf'.

'Sorry, Nick. I told you, you are exactly like our Doruf'.

'Lisie, I'll show you something. I've a tattoo with my wife's name, the first letter 'A'. You'll believe me now'.

He pulled off his clothes from his shoulder to show her the tattoo. It was dark green, but to his wonder the tattoo wasn't there. Like the time vanished, like Ann vanished the tattoo went somewhere. He checked his shoulders again and again but what he saw remained the same, absolute mystery.

'I don't see any tattoo. It is just your skin'

'I can't believe this, I am not where I should be, I am not in the time of my real life, I am not even in my body. Lisie, help me, Oh God, help me. I want to go back, I want to see my Ann'. He broke into tears.

'We'll find her Nick, we'll. Don't cry, don't worry'.

'No, we can't. I know that'

'Nick, there is always a solution'

'Lisie, this isn't the case. There is no way out here. I am trapped in time'.

Lisie looked at him, she didn't want to be like others who

believed Doruf went mad. Lisie wanted to trust his words, she wanted to be beside him in his problem to find a solution. She couldn't bear seeing him cry, seeing his tears made her very weak. Nick wasn't ready to believe the existence of this world, he was sure that the world has moved on very far to the year of 2014. He knew the world had witnessed many events between 1914 and 2014, so many things have changed in the world in this time. Technology, Communication mediums even the distance between the corners of the world was cut down drastically with the modern travel facilities. Nick told his mind that he is trapped in the past, the times of dead, times of forgotten days. He wanted to touch Lisie, he wanted to make sure she was alive. He took her hands quickly, he thought she would be frightened but she remained calm when he grabbed her hands. He tried to feel her body heat, the warmth of her blood. She looked into his eyes; she was observing his actions in a shock. Nick touched her face, both her cheeks with his hands. She stood silent and let him touch her body; she didn't find it disgraceful because he was her Doruf even though he didn't believe that yet.

'You are real, everything is real. It's just me, I do not exist'

Lisie couldn't take it anymore, she said with her wet eyes,

'Doruf, you are real. You are Doruf, my Doruf'.

She embraced him with all her love and kissed him several times all over his face. She asked him,

'Don't you remember me? Don't you remember we are

61

engaged?'

Asking him that she kissed his lips with her eyes closed and she kissed him for a long time. Her hands were around his neck and his hands were still over her cheeks. In such moments time always wanted to stand still, against the inevitable flow of nature. But Nick pulled her gently away; he couldn't enjoy her love because he was still confused. He wanted to be with Andria and not with Lisie. Lisie understood why he pushed her away. It didn't break her heart, she asked him,

'You still think you are not my Doruf. I accept that, but tell me who you are? Where do you live? And what do you mean when you say you're trapped in time?', She was calm but her words were determined, she wanted to end this uncertainty forever.

'If you tell me, you are free. I'll believe you're not the Doruf I know or I'll love you, I'll love you forever'.

Nick felt a compassion for her. He was able to understand her situation. He knew how painful it was for him to think he lost his Ann. He could see in her eyes the same pain, pain of losing Doruf whom she loved the most. Nick didn't want her to feel that way, he was sure he wasn't himself. He knew he was somewhere he doesn't belong, but he was sure somebody belonged here in the name of Doruf. He was certain he overtook Doruf somehow. He knew Lisie deserved Doruf without his permission. Nick was helpless there to find Andria because Ann was beyond the hands of human; she was in the twentieth century England; that meant she was in the future of this world where Lisie loved Doruf. Ann was exactly a hundred years ahead in the future where she was living with Nick, or supposed to live.

'Lisie, take me out. Let's go somewhere, I'll tell you my story. I should tell you beforehand, each word I say will be truth. You should believe me and please don't ask me to prove anything, I don't even have my identity. You should believe me just as my words.'

Lisie took him out; she showed him the country roads across the cornfields. Nick unveiled his life before Lisie. He told him everything about Andria, how they met, their marriage, life in London, what they did for living, their new house in Coventry and even the night before he woke up into an unfamiliar place without even his own identity. Lisie and Nick were sitting beside the Sava River, the river was silent and cold. There were some swans swimming, they didn't bother about Lisie and Nick sitting there as if they knew them very well. Early sun light and breeze and the light noises the swans made, there was nothing there to disturb them.

'Believe me, you are my Doruf'

'I know I'm your Doruf. I see that Lisie, but I don't remember you or anything of this place. I am living in your Doruf with the memories of my own life in 2014. I came here from the future, someone took me here for something, I still don't know what they want. My heart belongs to my wife, she is not even born if you think from your time of life'.

Nick continued,

'But I know she is there, I know future is somewhere very close to us but beyond our eyes. I've seen it, I lived there, I belong there. I travelled through time, I am a time traveller.'

Sava River holds the mirror

Solemnity and an irresistible compassion towards each other among Lisie and Doruf filled up arena of Sava River. Even though Nick didn't want to completely welcome Doruf back into life, his existence was accepted in this world as Nick was a mare possible future. Human will is a very thin line of security when it is up against the will of nature and situations. Nick began to see the beauty of Lisie, her eyes, lips, her hair and its aroma. His senses finally sensed her beauty while they were all by themselves in the lake side. He was slowly falling in love with her; he wanted her by his side to weep for his loss of love while Lisie was falling in love with Nick and Doruf, her love for Doruf pushed her to love Nick. She was in a love triangle. Nick walked closer to the lake to see his face, to see the face of Doruf. Lake was still, it always was very still in the mornings. He saw himself in the water. His face seemed very new and strange. Nick didn't feel that he was seeing his reflection, he felt he was meeting another person somewhere out in his lifetime. He whispered himself,

'Look at him, this is strange. I see a new face, a new world, his world'

Nick turned his face from the river, he didn't want to see him anymore. But Lisie touched his shoulder and gave him confidence to feel the new world, the new life he met with.

'Don't turn back your face from the truth. See yourself'.

'No, I can't. It's not my face, it's not my world'

'Don't say that Nick, my world is living through you. Doruf is my life'

He couldn't neglect her plea, he looked into her eyes. He saw an ocean of helplessness in them. He was sure even after looking at the reflection of Doruf's face he wouldn't be able to do anything to help her but he agreed. He looked into the lake and observed his own reflection. He had a thin beard grown and light brown hair cut short. His face told he had worked under sun a lot in summers but his face muscles were stronger than his own. He was absolutely different from the face he had when he was Nick, Doruf looked handsome and very young. Nick called the reflection with the name, 'Doruf'. He turned his face towards Lisie and asked her,

'How old is he? Doruf?'

'Twenty five, he is two years older than me'

Nick shook his head with a sigh and told,

'He is five years younger than me'

Lisie smiled but it was just a partial smile, she couldn't smile because she knew what was going through Nick's mind.

'I know a woman, she does magic, some say she can tell future', she paused for a while and continued,

'She might be able to solve this problem; she might send you back to your time'

'It is not back in time, it is ahead. It is a hundred years ahead in future. I don't think I would meet Ann again'

His legs were unable to carry his body in balance. He was slipping in over anxiety. Before he fell into the lake Lisie held him closer without letting him slip. She hugged him and tried to console his weary thoughts.

'I am here; don't think you are alone'

Nick hugged her and shed his worries, anxiety and his fear over Lisie's shoulder and hair. Lisie didn't stop him, she was speechless. She knew it would be better if she let him to cry all his pain. She gently moved her hands over his back and shoulders, she didn't say a single word till he wiped off tears from his face. He stood away from Lisie as if he didn't want to share his feelings with Lisie. But she had no complaints about it, she understood Nick's position too.

'I'm sure she can help you, I can take you there. It's a little far from here. A full day ride to reach her place. My mother knew her very well, they were very close. She was at mom's funeral. She sensed mommy's death even though we didn't tell'

Nick was paying attention when she began to tell about the supernatural powers of the Gypsy woman. Nick's eyes were pointed to Lisie's face. They told Lisie in silence that he wanted to hear more about the woman. Lisie continued when she saw it in him. 'She is not like us', Lisie said.

'She has powers. When she came for mother's funeral she told us that she was informed about my mother's death by my mother herself. She said my mother visited her before her soul left the body forever, just to say it's her time to go'.

'And?', Nick wanted to hear more about her.

'What makes it more unbelievable is mother had no trouble when she died. She was very healthy. She was sleeping by my side, she didn't even make any sound that night. And in the morning, before we took her to the cemetery Dorika reached here'.

'Oh, that's strange'

'Yes, she is strange. She told me before she left to Avala that she won't die a normal death. She said, she will disappear from the world before it consumes her life. She says death is a transformation of energy'.

'I should meet her. She can help me'

'Yes, I'll take you there. But no one here should know where we go. No one likes her'.

'Why?'

'Because she is different, everyone expects everyone to be same. Difference means something new, people are afraid of the new'.

Lisie stopped talking for a while and gazed at the western horizon, her face was filled with curiosity and a light smile flavoured with anxiety and disbelief. Nick sat beside her and asked,

'What are you thinking?'

'Nothing, it's just this situation. You are here with me in the body of my Fiancé but you say you are from the future. You say you lived in London in 2000's but we are in 1914 and we think future is yet to come'. She looked at his face and smiled with her curious eyes.

'You talk about our future as it is past. It's strange; people will call you a mad man if you say this to anyone else. It's my love for Doruf that made me believe your words. I am sitting with another man from another century, yet feels like sitting with him. We sat here yesterday after his work in the farm. But in one night he changed, he became you. He became a stranger to me even when his living body is here walking with me. Your mind came in him and his mind went out somewhere. You lost your love and I lost the mind that loved me, in the gap of one night'.

One drop of tear flowed from her right eye but Nick

consoled her,

'Don't worry Lisie. You still have his body. You can see him, you can still touch him, hug him and kiss him. You still have the place you belong and your own people. In a way you still have everything'.

'You have me, Nick'. She said holding his left hand,

'You are not alone, you have my love'

She kissed him on his lips and hugged him sitting close. Nick wasn't able to resist her love, even though Lisie was new in his life she deserved him and he deserved her love. Nick was falling in love with Lisie even when memory of his Ann was alive in him. He didn't want to cheat Andria, who loved him more than anything in the world around her. He gently pushed Lisie away from him and without looking at her face he said,

'I can't do this Lisie, I can't let myself to fall in love with you. Ann wouldn't do this to me'.

'Lisie smiled and told him,

'I love you because you're my Doruf and somehow I know even Nick belongs to my heart. I love my Dorf and I've fallen in love with my Dorf's new mind, Nick. Now I love both of you'

'I don't feel it that way Lisie, you're very beautiful and very young. You definitely tempt my desire to fall in love but I would regret this if I ever go back to Ann. Let me stay

Andria's husband'.

'You're a nice person. You will definitely get your wife back'

'I'm sorry Lisie, are you hurt?'

'I'm, but I see the same attitude of Doruf in you. He'll do the same if he is in your place'.

Determined to meet the supernatural

They had to travel a long way to the Avala mountain ranges to meet Dorika. It was not easy to travel in those days that far especially when the whole country was covered up in an unexpected snowfall. It wasn't winter yet, it was just July. It was supposed to be hot during July and August in the country. But last night surprised everyone with an unwelcome snowfall. It covered up their corns and vegetation but luckily the morning came with enough sunlight and slowly melted the remains of the snow. Lisie and Nick decided to travel to Avala as early as possible. Lisie knew how to reach Avala, but the roads were not frequented with travellers, it was a rural road commonly used by horse riders. Lisie persuaded her father and her step mother to let her travel to Avala with Nick, but her parents had no idea that Nick was actually Nick. In their eyes he was Doruf. Lisie's father asked him whether he was well enough to travel a long way.

'Doruf, how do you feel now? Take rest for a few days'

'Papa, I am with him. He is okay'. Lisie interrupted her father as he was intended to talk with Nick. Nick didn't know how to talk in Hungarian, but if Lisie's parents understand that they would still think that Doruf is not well. Lisie managed to cover up Doruf's loss of identity.

'Stay at Svetozar, they have cottages for travellers. Don't ride in the night, those roads are lonely. Doruf, take care of Lisie'

Nick couldn't accept when Lisie's father called him Doruf. But he had to accept and act like he was Doruf. He tried to respond in the little Hungarian Lisie taught him, he said,

'Igen', which meant 'Yes'.

They started their journey to Avala Mountains on Lisie's horse. On their way Lisie told Nick,

'Nick, you never rode a horse before? It's a shame, Doruf knows it very well'

She looked at his face and smiled to see his reaction, she could only see half of his face as he was sitting behind her.

'Well, I can ride a car. I own a Ferrari. It's not here anyway'.

'So what, you need my horse now. But what is a Ferrari?'

'Oh, it's a shame you don't even know the name', he tried to tease her in return. That's exactly what Lisie wanted. She wanted to loosen his stress. Lisie looked at him in amazement; her eyes seemed calm seeing his smile. It was Nick's responsibility to Lisie to explain what a Ferrari was. He said,

'Lisie, it's a luxury car, a very expensive car'.

'Is it faster than the Army patrol jeeps?'

'Yes, it must be. It is Italian by origin. It was made in Italy. I don't know when they started their company. If I had my mobile phone I could have checked it on the internet'

Lisie looked at him, she didn't have any idea about mobile phones and she had no idea about Internet too. There was no wonder, she belonged to the beginning of the twentieth century and nick belonged to a much technologically advanced twenty first century. Nick felt sorry for Lisie for dragging her into the complicated ideas of another century. But she was not ready to give up.

'What is mobile phone? What does it do with that net?'

'Lisie, do you know a telephone? The thing in which you can talk with people?'

'Yes, I know it. But I never saw a real one'.

'Mobile phone does the same, you can talk with people. Unlike the telephones, they have no wires connected. The voice is sent through air. With a mobile phone you can go everywhere and talk with everyone anywhere in the world. Modern mobiles can take photos, send photos, talk with people seeing their faces with the help of Internet. It is a lot different from your time Lisie'.

'Internet?'

'That's something you can't see with your eyes. It is information collected and saved like in the books. But instead of books it is saved in invisible man made space. Advanced technology would help you to collect data from there with phones and other similar machines'

'How is it possible?', Lisie became curious about the extraordinary technology Nick explained.

'Don't know Lisie, I am just a business man. Only experts of internet can answer that question. I can tell you an example, Internet is like God, you ask anything to it and the answer is right there. For example you ask about your country, you will get all information'.

Lisie smiled at him, she said,

'Now you sound like a mad man talking nonsense. But I trust you, the world is changing so quickly'.

'Yes, after the world wars everything changed so quickly'

'World War?', Lisie was terrified hearing about a world war. She knew about wars between neighbouring countries for land and their own issues. But she had no idea about a war called world war. She asked him in disbelief.

'What do you mean with World Wars?'

'World War happened twice, Lisie. Almost the entire world fought against each other. Soviets, British, Germans, French, Americans, Japanese even soldiers from the colonies of each super powers fought in the World Wars, millions were killed'.

'Don't talk about this please. I don't want to hear it'.

'Sorry, sorry Lisie. I didn't mean to scare you',

Nick forgot to think from the side of those people. To him it was a finished story, just a forgotten history. But for them it was their present life, they were yet to witness the fury of destruction. He looked at her face that became pale white in the fear he injected into her veins. Suddenly a thought sparked in his mind, it was the date in the newspaper. He recollected the date that was currently his present day, June 17, 1914. He remembered the lessons he learnt from his childhood. He knew the world war broke out in the year 1914, his current year. He understood that the world war was very close to them. He knew it very well that it started with the invasion of Serbia by the Empire of Austria-Hungary. He couldn't remember the exact date of the invasion, but he knew it was one month after the assassination of Archduke Franz Ferdinand the heir of the Austrian throne. He knew he was spending his life with Lisie in the soil of Serbia. He didn't have to think a lot to realise the danger mounting up against the lives of those poor villagers. He was least concerned with his life as it meant nothing to him at that point. Nick asked Lisie to stop the horse as he felt very weak, he wanted to tell everything to her. But something stopped him, he didn't tell her about the advancing danger. He didn't want to push her into the ditch of panic.

'What happened Doruf?', she asked and corrected herself in the next sentence. 'Sorry, what happened Nick? Are you sick again?'

'No, I am Okay Lisie. I want some water. I am not familiar with travelling on horses. I think that is my problem. Let's walk a little distance'.

As the journey continues

Nick was in serious distress. He felt uncomfortable when hiding a great disaster awaiting her country and even her life. If he reveals her about the destruction world war unleashed, he knew she would have to spend the rest of her days in fear. She was just twenty three, a simple villager just starting to live her life. He didn't know how to expose poor Lisie to the terrible days coming. Yet he knew it was an undeniable reality. But he had it determined in his mind not to reveal anything to Lisie.

He was not worried about his life if the war was about to swallow him. Because without Andria, without anything he knew as his own, without even his body, he was already dead there. Nick's personality was viewed as a mere psychiatric problem within the mind of Doruf. In psychiatric terms, Doruf's personality disorder resulted in the identity of Nick. No one even bothered to listen to his words except Lisie. Out of her love towards Doruf she heard his words and trusted him. It was just because Nick was an invisible identity and Doruf was a physical reality which she could touch, see and love. She proved herself exceptional when she opted to follow the invisible. Perhaps she followed the invisible to regain the physical form of her love, Doruf. Lisie gave him resort when everything turned upside down. It was his turn now to keep her happy at all costs. He wasn't sure how dreadful would be the presents the war offers for Lisie. But he wanted her not to know anything about it. It is definitely absurd to live knowing the exact last moment of one's life. Certainty is a security in most of the cases but it takes away the ecstasy of riding strange roads when it comes to the journey of our life.

They walked together about half a mile. Lisie knew they had to travel a long way to reach Avala. It was not possible to travel through the lonely roads in the night. As Lisie's father told they planned to stay at Svetozar. It was already the middle of the day. To reach Svetozar before it becomes too late in the night, they had to hurry. Lisie's horse Kaiser was a very strong male horse. Kaiser wouldn't find it difficult to travel a long distance if Lisie pushes him. His black colour definitely was even darker than a moonless night of the Serbian woods. Lisie didn't take her hands off Doruf's hands. She thought he needed her care throughout their trip to Avala. Kaiser walked slowly and followed Lisie and Doruf as if he was ought to follow them wherever they go. But at times Kaiser tend to stop and check the narrow road to the end of his eye sight chewing tiny grass tops he found on his way. As they moved on Kaiser suddenly stopped with a whine. Lisie turned around to check what happened with Kaiser. He showed his distress by shaking his head and standing on his two legs to show he was ready to face something.

Lisie grabbed tight on his harness to control him, she raised her voice,

'Kaiser, calm down. Kaiser'

He became calm when Lisie raised her voice but Lisie was sure that something took his attention on the road. She looked at the end of the road, she was checking whether there was anything dangerous. She was afraid of the wolves, but they never came across men especially in the days. She told Nick,

'There is something terrifying Kaiser. It could be wolf'.

'Oh my God' Nick couldn't believe he had to face a wolf face to face. He asked her,

'Do you have something to scare them?'

Lisie looked at his face; she could see it in his eyes that he was scared to death. She smiled at him. She was afraid for sure but she lived there for twenty three years, hearing about the wolves, seeing them and sometimes even facing them. She told Nick,

'You'll see'

She untied a leather pouch that was fastened to the side of her horse. When the leather roll was opened before Nick's eyes he felt that he was accompanying a young wild pirate all these time. On that leather roll there were three sharp knives and a pair of old model pistols. Nick looked at her in disbelief, he asked her without taking his eyes off from her pistols.

'Who are you people? Are you really farmers?'

'Common, on the horse', she asked him to get himself on the horse.

'Are we going to move on?'

'Yes, it is normal here. It will be okay'.

'Are you sure? I'm scared to hell.'

'It happens a lot here, they will go away'.

She gently shook Kaiser's harness and told him,

'Kaiser, move'

She wanted to bring down Nick's tension; she told him what

79

really bothered her at that point.

'I have to focus on talking English when I speak with you, and change to Hungarian when talking with Kaiser. It is difficult for me. Learn some Hungarian on our way Nick, English is difficult for Kaiser'.

'Lisie, don't talk. The wolf will find us'.

Lisie understood that nothing would change his mind. She asked him,

'Can you use a gun? Take the other gun'

'No, I can't. I have never used a gun'

'It is loaded. Just shoot when you see the wolf'.

'Is it legal?'

'Nick, you don't have to kill the wolf. Just shoot and it will run for its life'

'Are you sure?'

Lisie laughed gently,

'Yes, Nick. We do it all the time'.

Kaiser began to run faster to get away from the wolves. It was difficult for Nick to stay steady on the fast running horse. He said it aloud,

'Lisie, slow him down. Slow him down'

'Hold tight around me. He won't stop; he is trying to run away from them. Hold tight Nick'

'Oh my God, I can't stay steady'

Lisie took both his hands and quickly tightened them around her body.

'Nick, just hug me tighter. Close your eyes if you are afraid of speed'

Kaiser ran faster, nick felt the ground shaking with Kaiser's force. Nick opened his eyes to see whether the wolves were following them. He saw the trees passing by on both sides and the distant village road rushing towards them. Those roads were not straight, Kaiser took turns rapidly. Nick had a Ferrari as his own when he lived in England but he never rode it rough like this and he knew he would never. He didn't want to keep his eyes open as Kaiser was not ready to slow down. Nick could only hear the echoes of the horse's steps in the woods for a few more minutes. He was sure that they had already passed a long way with that speed. All of a sudden the echoes stopped; there was only wind as if they were passing through a lifeless desert. Nick opened his eyes to see where he was. As he expected it was a vast land with only a few tiny bushes and shapeless rocks.

'Where are we?', he spoke aloud to make his question audible for Lisie.

'We are reaching Sanad, after this dry area'.

'Would they follow us?', Nick was still stuck with the danger of wolves.

'They didn't follow us. They can't catch up with Kaiser, they know it'

'Then slow him down, Lisie. We are going so fast'.

Lisie pulled Kaiser on his harness, Kaiser slowed his speed. Lisie stroked on Kaiser's furry back as applause for the great effort he took for all three of them. Nick was still not ready to loosen his hands those were crossed around Lisie's body. Lisie asked him humorously with laughter on her face,

'Nick, how is my Ferrari?'

She knew what would be his reaction. He said,

'Crazier than mine, I wouldn't dare riding this'

'My father presented him on my birthday. He is super powerful'.

'I felt it'

'You are still hugging me, Nick', Lisie reminded him.

'Oh, I don't want to loosen my arms'

'You don't have to, you are my Doruf anyway'

Nick looked around the landscape. He liked the Serbian planes with tiny bushes and light yellow leaves dancing to the end of his sight. Those places reminded him of the country sides of Britain in the summer season. But the air smelled different perhaps with the different variety of plants. The end of the road narrowed into the vast cornfields that grew thick with the surplus sunlight and occasional rain.

'Lisie, I like your country. It is beautiful with its simplicity. I wish the world stayed like this forever'.

'Don't you like it there in England?'

'It's not anything to do with England Lisie, it is the whole world in the two thousands. It is too busy, unhealthy, it is a lot different from your life' He sighed looking skywards. His eyes seemed wet as he continued his words, 'But I belong there'.

'We will ask her to help you with your problem. That's why we travel to Avala. Don't worry Nick'.

He smiled at her as she turned around. He told,

'You are my only friend here'

Lisie smiled back and asked him to do her a favour. She wanted to hear more about the life in the two thousands. She asked him,

'Nick, would you tell me more about your time?'

'Yes, what do you want to know about the world?'

'Everything'

Two thousands are definitely different

What is the meaning of keeping everything very personal? What actually is time? How real are we? When the existence of everything including ourselves starts to be in suspicion, time does not count, feelings do not count and places as well. Only one thing that bothers at that point is the question, 'how it began?' Everything is balanced between each other with an impeccable accuracy to give us a feeling that they are real. Like a beam of light trapped inside a diamond everything is trapped in the feeling of existence.

Lisie asked Nick,

'I want to know about Ann, would you tell me?'

'My wife?'

'Yes'.

He cleared his throat and looked at Lisie's face. She didn't look at him even though she knew his eyes were watching her. She kept her eyes straight on the road, as if she was focused on riding. Nick tried to talk about Andria attempting to leave behind his unwillingness.

'Okay, okay. So, Ann...she is' he struggled to speak about her. 'She is, she and I were engaged in 2009. And we got married in 2011. We were so happy, so happy that day'

Lisie turned around and smiled at him. Nick was still holding onto Lisie's body as if he was hugging her. Lisie told him,

'Then?', she wanted to know more.

'She was from Coventry. She liked it there as always. I was 27 and she was 25 when we married. And Lisie, we met each other when I went to Coventry University for higher studies. I liked her at the moment when I first saw her. Not because of her beautiful face, but because of her beautiful personality'. A light smile bloomed on his cheeks as he became talkative about his wife. He recollected the days when he was a university student doing his post graduation.

'I was doing my post graduation in business administration. Coventry University was popular among international students as well. It was 2009 and it was summer vacation for us. We were not free because we had to prepare our thesis for the final semester. But I was always lazy, leaving my work for the last moment. As always I went out with my good friends for some drinks at Quids Inn, it was right opposite the university. We were beer buddies mostly but we decided to get a little more than just a beer that evening. We went on with some shots and a few cocktails and we spent around three hours in the pub. When it was around 9:00 O'clock in the evening I decided to head back to my apartment. On my way I saw this young beautiful girl walking into the university library. She was talking with someone on her phone with a charming smile. I wanted to know her name and I just followed her in the library till she turned around and stared at me. I could see in her eyes all her anger and fear'

Lisie giggled hearing his story. But she added her opinion,

'Oh Nick, you know it can scare a girl especially when it is a drunk man that she was up to'.

'I know, but I did it. That was not nice from my side'.

'And what happened?', Lisie hurried to hear more.

'And then she asked me why I followed her. I had no answer Lisie. My first impression was broken into thousand pieces. But I had to say something to cover up my mistake. I didn't lie, I told her the fact that I was actually following her'

'Then'

'She asked me what I wanted. I told her that I wanted to know her name'. As Nick was talking about his first meeting with Andria, Lisie's face became delighted with the interesting clash between them. Nick continued,

'She asked me why I wanted to know her name. I didn't have a polished answer again, so I told her the truth. I said I liked her. She was not happy with that answer she went on questioning me. She nodded her head in distress. She doubted me as I didn't even know her. She asked how I could like her without any idea about her. Her questions left me helpless in cooking up a story. I had to tell the very honest answers. I told her that I liked her smile. By then some students and some library staff began to notice us. To reduce our voice, she came closer and went on with her concerns. She said that I scared her a lot especially when I jumped into the elevator with her. At the end she asked me my name. I told her my name and to prove her that I was not cooking up a fake name I showed her my university identity card. It was embarrassing but the alcohol helped me to withstand the shame. I looked at everyone and told that everything was alright. But she didn't tell me her name. She told me if I really wanted to know her name meet her the next day in the library. I asked her why did she do that and she made it clear that I was a little drunk. She was stubborn, she didn't tell anything about her that evening'.

Lisie heard their story; she liked how Andria tested Nick. Lisie looked at Nick's face. She said,

'I like her. So did you go to meet her?'

'Yes, the next evening I went to the library'

'Didn't she come?'

'She came, yes. We talked about each other for about an hour. I liked the way we talked in whispers as we had to maintain the silence in the library. She was doing her bachelor degree in Accounting and Finance in the university'.

'Then you engaged?'

'No, we were meeting each other a few weeks and only then she accepted to come with me for a date. Somehow, we proved that we were meant for each other. And on the Christmas day I proposed her when we were in London with my family'.

'Excellent, excellent', Lisie was satisfied.

They were passing a street busy with people. It was a town with a few shops, barns and some old fashioned hotels. Nick asked Lisie where they were.

'Padej', she told him in her Hungarian accent. But she wasn't finished with Andria. She said,

'Nick. When you meet her tell her I liked how you met each other'.

Nick's eyes were filled with tears hearing that. He wasn't sure about meeting Ann.

'I hope I can see her again Lisie. I don't know'.

Lisie knew his pain, she said,

'I promise you Nick, Dorika would find a solution. She will tell you what happened to you'. Her eyes were looking around the streets for a less crowded shop. She pointed to one shop,

'Nick, let's go there. I am thirsty. We need to buy some apples as well. It is a long journey'.

'Alright, let's go in. I am also thirsty'.

Kaiser stopped there. Lisie walked into the shop. She took both her pistols into the shop hiding them under her waistcoat. She didn't want them to be stolen otherwise she had no plan to take them into the shop. Nick saw what she hid under her coat he looked around in distress to check whether somebody noticed her. Lisie turned her face towards him,

'Nick, come'.

They went into the shop. It was arranged neatly, there were places for visitors to relax. Those wooden chairs and tables looked old but they gave a classic atmosphere. There were a few paintings decorating the walls. Smell of wine and fresh baked bread was filled in the air and noises of plates and spoons faintly echoed inside the shop. That was one of the finest restaurants in the village of Padej. Somebody approached Lisie and Nick as they set themselves at a corner.

'Hello, Madam. What would you like to taste from our wonderful restaurant?'

He was the owner of the restaurant and he wanted to make sure his customers were always pleased with their service. He spoke in Hungarian to Lisie. Nick patiently remained on his chair letting Lisie to talk.

'Hello, two beer please'

'What would you like to eat, we have made something special today. We have Turkish Moussaka'. He introduced the name of his special item 'Turkish Moussaka' very slowly like a street magician announcing the name of his best trick to the crowd.

'Hmm, Moussaka. That's nice', Lisie looked at Nick. She was sure Nick didn't understand what she was talking with the man. Nick remained silent as he didn't want to show him that he doesn't speak Hungarian.

'We want to try your Moussaka. Please get some for both of us', Lisie told him. As he was taking notes on his pocket diary Lisie asked him.

'What is your name?'

'I'm Daniel, this is my restaurant madam'.

'Ah! Nice place Daniel'

'Thank you madam, let me get your order very quickly'

He smiled at both of them before hurrying to the kitchen.

Lisie explained everything to Nick. Nick was wondering about the taste of Turkish Moussaka. Lisie had already given him a brief explanation about the ingredients of the dish. Lisie waved her hands gently to catch Daniel's attention. She wanted to order something else. As Daniel approached Lisie told him,

'Please get us two cups of fish soup too'

'Alright Madam, soups are ready. I will get them now. I recommend you start with the soup then'.

'Perfect. Thank you, Daniel'. Lisie smiled at him politely. And she asked him whether they had something for her horse. Daniel had nothing in his restaurant for Kaiser. He said,

'I am sorry Madam, we don't have it here. But you will find a shop at the end of this street. They have everything you might need. They sell horse food, oats, hay, green grass and carrots as well if your horse prefer. It's my friend Josif's shop'.

'That's okay Daniel, I will get it from there'.

Daniel went back to the kitchen to get their soup.

They enjoyed their meal in the local restaurant of Padej. Daniel served them well adding two more customers in his list completely satisfied with the service and food he provided. They spent about half an hour at Deniel's restaurant. Then they continued their journey to the Avala Mountain. They didn't forget to give some oats, hay and enough water for Kaiser at Josif's shop. Melenci was around 30 miles away from Padej as Josif told them. Lisie had a vague calculation that it would take Kaiser around five hours if he walked slowly with some rest in each one hour. She knew it was a little too much for Kaiser and for them to travel that far in one day but they had no choice. They had to hurry. Village roads of Padej presented themselves with beautiful scenes of farms and farmers. Both sides of the roads were covered with cornfields and sunflowers. At some places herds of cattle were seen inside large areas blocked with wooden fence and matted with green grass. Some places had only a few houses in the middle of their farms and some closer to the roads. Nick liked the ride even when he knew that he was trapped in the past within those spectacular sites of country life.

Kaiser rode over many villages and old towns like I oš , Bo ar, Karlovo, Be ej and Kumane before he reached the soil of Melenci. I oš was more lively compared to other areas they passed. There were a lot of houses. Most of them were Serb farmers. Kids playing on the streets of I oš waved their hands at Nick and Lisie as if they were familiar with travellers from other villages and towns. It was starting to get darker when Melenci welcomed Lisie and Nick. They were both tired. They were eager to find a place to rest. Like birds flying over the farmlands to their nests they rode through the roads seeking their shelter. As they were passing through a less crowded street Lisie noticed an old building with a large board exposed at its door. It was written in Serbian and Hungarian. The electric lamps that lightened the building seemed very old to the eyes of Nick. They reminded him with their less bright yellowish light that he belonged to a different brighter world. Lisie pulled Kaiser's leather strap. He gently stopped there and shook his head a few times as he already knew that it was finally some time to rest and sleep.

'Nick it looks like an affordable tavern. Let's stay here tonight', Lisie told him.

Nick looked at the building. He was satisfied with the look of the tavern as it was neatly maintained. He told her,

'Hmm...This is fine. So this is Melenci'.

'Yes. It is Melenci, finally', Lisie breathed out a little aloud showing her exhaustion of the long ride. It was a very long journey even for Kaiser as he was not used to long rides. They had already travelled around fifty miles from Bari to reach Melency and they had to travel another sixty miles to reach Avala Mountain where Dorika lived in her cottage all by herself.

Lisie stepped into the tavern to check whether they would be given a room for the night. Nick waited outside with Kaiser till she came back.

'We can stay here, they have rooms available', she came back saying this. Somebody was following Lisie. He came out with her from the tavern and smiled at Nick. Lisie asked him to take Kaiser to their barn. She asked him to feed her horse properly without any delay as she knew he would be tired carrying them a long way throughout the day. Before he started to walk towards the barn he introduced himself to his new guests. This time Nick grasped the meaning of the Hungarian they spoke.

'I am Ambrus. Please wait at the hall. I will come now'

'Okay, Ambrus. We will wait'.

They walked into the tavern and waited for Ambrus.

The Tavern and the Evening of Music

1914, Melenci, Serbia

Evenings in that tavern were normally quite. But that evening was special, they had some musicians as their guests. They were a group, wandering all around the country performing at different villages and towns. They made others happy with their music; it was their way of life. Life often introduces different personalities. Some would care about making themselves happy and some others would try to make others happy. But rarely does it introduce another kind who perhaps forgot themselves while trying to make others happy.

There were singers, trumpeters, flute musicians, drummers and more, they stayed at Melenci for about a week. Nick and Lisie were lucky to witness their performance because the music was magical and mind blowing. The musicians didn't play their instruments too loud; they played soft music especially romantic songs. They didn't want anyone to be disturbed in their comfortable sleeps. They tried their best to keep their music inside the lobby of the tavern. It was not their performance. It was just their practice before their next performance near the local church of Melenci.

Nick and Lisie sat in the lobby hearing them play their music.

The whole area was influenced with their light music as even in the air the vibrations of their trumpets could be felt. The musicians had no problem with Lisie and Nick listening to their practice instead they were happy to see them enjoy their melody. One of the musicians, who played the lute kept his eyes at Lisie's face when his fingers moved quickly between the strings of the lute. He didn't take his eyes away from Lisie for a long time. Lisie noticed him; he was young with neatly shaped thin moustache and beard. He had long hair that danced along with the movements of his fingers. Lisie didn't want to give him an impression that she was noticing him. She had avoided many youngsters who were all seeking her love. She did it because she loved only Doruf and she wasn't ready to fall in an unnecessary relationship with anyone else. But time pushed her beyond the limits of human beings making her to love Nick while Doruf's mind was replaced with the mind of Nick. Her situation was strange, she loved Doruf. She was still with him. She could touch him, kiss him and hug him. But while doing these she was falling in love with Nick's mind. She couldn't avoid her temptation to cuddle Doruf. But she knew while holding Doruf in her arms that she was embracing the mind of Nick, who was husband to Andria. This is a strange circumstance that dragged her into this triangular love, something she couldn't resist. But the case of this young musician was different. It must be avoided to remain Doruf's faithful lover.

As the song was finished, the young lute player slowly walked towards Lisie, he still had his lute in his hands. Lisie was uncomfortable, she didn't want somebody to woo on her in front of Doruf's eyes. She didn't know how Nick would react if something goes wrong. The young man came closer to Lisie and Nick with a smile on his face. He started talking to Lisie,

'Hello, I didn't mean to offend you. I saw you enjoying the music. That's why I looked at you while playing. I guess it was my mistake. I was lost in the music'.

Lisie didn't know what to say. She felt embarrassed as he read through her mind. She knew she made him feel humiliated at least a little bit. She wanted to apologize for misunderstanding his eyes. But no words came out of her tongue. She struggled to talk, but at last she told him,

'No, no, it was silly of me. I behaved so silly'.

Nick remained calm even though he didn't understand the conversation between Lisie and the musician. But the Musician smiled at him and Nick's politeness forced him to give a smile in return.

'Is he your husband?', the musician asked Lise.

'Not yet, but soon. We are engaged', she showed her engagement ring to the musician. And the musician introduced himself to Nick. He said,

'Hello Sir, I am Dimitri'.

Nick smiled, but before he told anything Lisie took over. She said,

'He's Nick and I am Lisie. We enjoyed your music a lot. It was extraordinary'.

'Thank you, I am glad you enjoyed it. Well, I need to go back. We need to finish more songs'.

He went back to the other musicians and continued playing. Lisie and Nick remained there listening to their songs until they finished practising. It was around ten o'clock in the night by then. Nick and Lisie went back to their rooms after having a small chat with Dimitri and other musicians. They were both relaxed listening to the music for more than an hour at the lobby. Sleep rushed into their eyes, they slept in the same room on same bed.

Second Day of the Journey

1914, Melenci, Serbia

Ambrus brought Kaiser to the front gate early in the morning. He was sleeping comfortable when Lisie and Nick vacated their room to continue their trip to Avala. But Ambrus had no problem with it as it was usual in his life. He had to wake up from his sweet dreams for countless times to help the guests in the tavern. Sometimes he hardly gets time to rest when the tavern becomes filled with guests.

'Where are you going sir? It is very early in the morning. It is still cold. I think you have to travel a long way'.

Ambrus talked to Nick in his colloquial tone. He didn't look at Nick's face even though he was expecting his reply. He was busy with filling tobacco in his pipe. Ambrus threw his woollen scarf around his neck before he lit the pipe. He eagerly swallowed a few puffs to fill his lungs and slowly released circles of smoke through his mouth. Lisie replied Ambrus,

'We are heading to Avala. We need to reach there before it gets too dark'. Lisie tried to repeat the same words she told everybody about Nick's silence. She said,

'He is my fiancé, Doruf. He is not well. He can't talk for some days'.

'What happened to him?'

'He had severe fever last week. It infected his throat. It is painful for him to talk'.

'Wish you a quick recovery sir. Don't forget to use some thick clothes, it is very cold. This is not good for your throat.'

Ambrus handed the leather harness of Kaiser to Lisie and gently patted on Kaiser's head. Kaiser shook his head when Ambrus stroke his face. Lisie noticed that and told Ambrus,

'I know you treated him very well. This is how he shows his gratitude. He likes you'

'I have, you are right. I like him too'. Ambrus told them farewell in his own way. He removed his hat and gently raised it above his head. As Kaiser started to move he told them,

'Visit us again, come in and say hello when you travel through these places'.

Lisie turned around and smiled at him. She was happy to know that Kaiser wasn't left alone in the barn. Thoughts about Kaiser didn't allow her to sleep peacefully in the night. She was thoughtful whether Kaiser was fed properly or whether he got a neat place to rest. She knew Kaiser wouldn't like the new place especially when she wasn't beside him. But seeing Kaiser's happiness while being with Ambrus told her everything. She didn't have to think a lot to figure out that Kaiser was satisfied with that new place.

There were some white poppy flowers on the sideways of the street smiling at them in the fading moonlight. They were shivering in the last wind of the night. Lisie pulled out her pocket watch and told Nick,

'It's six. We should reach enta before we stop for our lunch. Then we can cross Danube at Bor a. It is easier from there to Avala'.

Lisie and Nick managed to complete half of their journey in one day. They knew that their effort was almost near a success but they didn't know what Veronica prepared for them in their return. Veronica became blind with her envy towards Lisie. She couldn't forget the words Lisie threw at her face. She had already started sowing seeds of suspicion in the minds of Lisie's parents. She told Lisie's father Radmilo her concerns about Doruf. Radmilo didn't believe Veronica's words in the beginning because he knew Veronica very much. But Veronica's capacity to spark suspicions in somebody's mind worked well at last. Radmilo became worried about the future of his daughter's life when Veronica told him that Doruf lost his mind. She made him believe that Doruf's mental health would never recover. Veronica knew that it was not right to cause trouble in the lives of two innocent human beings but she loved herself to the point where she had to neglect her thoughts about being ethical. Veronica knew Lisie would cry all her life if she loses Doruf. That was the only result Veronica wanted from this sin.

Without knowing anything about this plan Lisie and Nick travelled, they talked about each other, ate together, relaxed listening to the music of the wandering troop and slept comfortably in a tavern at Melenci. They began this tiring journey with the hopes of solving a dilemma but in their absence another trouble rolled over to their lives.

Long cornfields, villages, people, tiny roads, woods and streams were all falling behind the steps of Kaiser. His hiss and the sound of his hooves became music for Nick and Lisie while riding across the lonely farmlands of many villages and towns. Sun poured enough heat for the cornfields to warm up from the lazy night. Rarely some motorcars passed them on their way. It was a time when not many owned motorcars. Horses and carts were very common especially among the farmers and middle class. But the sight of the old model motorcars and carts reminded Nick that he was lost in time. They also reminded him that he is Doruf for Lisie and others in that period. Lisie understood his situation very well and as if to reduce his tension she kept talking about everything that she found interesting. Lisie's attempts were not completely in vain because Nick forgot his problems at times. Sometimes he was so keen into the topics Lisie put forward. She told him about the life in Serbia, how they made their living, about Doruf, about their engagement, about their plan to start their life together. Nick and Lisie felt strange while talking about Doruf because whenever they mentioned about Doruf it indirectly pointed towards Nick. Nick told her while she became talkative about Doruf at an instance,

'Lisie, when you say you are planning to start living with Doruf, it actually means you are planning to be with me. It is so unreal. But that is happening to me for real'.

Lisie told him in reply,

'I know it is confusing. But you are very lucky. You have experienced two different centuries in one life. Your problem will be solved once we meet Dorika. And after you return to your wife, you can tell her that you have seen Serbia, you can tell her you met me, you can tell her that you lived here with us as my Doruf'.

Lisie gently laughed, but for some reason her eyes seemed dull. Nick had a smile on his face but he didn't see the change on her face. It was perhaps she didn't want him to see her immediate change. As they were passing by the Bega River at Zrenjanin Kaiser refused to walk. He showed his distress. Nick didn't understand his problem but Lisie knew everything about her horse. Even an unusual hiss from him made a meaningful communication between Lisie and Kaiser. She stroked his neck with her fingers and told him,

'I know, I know. We will do that'.

Nick wondered what was going on between them. It was uncomfortable for him when she talked with people in their language because he couldn't understand anything. And seeing her communicating with the horse did spark an uneasy feeling inside him. He asked Lisie,

'What, what happened to him? Is he tired'?

'He wants to drink from the river. I think we should stop for some time. Let him rest'.

Lisie helped Nick to get down from the horse before she got herself down. She told Kaiser a little louder,

'Kaiser, go for it. Do not wander around, stay close'.

He moved closer to the river very slowly. Lisie and Nick noticed a small hut a few yards away from them beside the river. It looked like a vendor's tiny shack. They both became curious about the shop as they couldn't find anybody near it. Its wide window was open. They could see some glass jars with some baked breads and nuts. They saw an empty chair inside the room that was very small but there was a burning pipe over the table spreading the smell of tobacco. It was enough to assume that somebody was there. As they approached the shack they heard somebody moving inside as if searching for something.

'Hello', Lisie broke the silence.

Hearing her voice an old man peeped out from under the table on which the glass jars were kept. As the jars were partially filled with the bread and nuts, they could see only his grey hair and eyes with wrinkles of age around them. He started talking with his shattering voice,

'Hello, please wait a minute. I was looking for my kettle'.

Lisie saw a kettle a little away from the jars. She asked him,

'Are you looking for this one'? Here is a kettle'. She pointed her finger towards the kettle on the table. The old man stood up to check it. With a smile on his face he looked at Lisie and told,

'I am on my seventy two. I am losing even my memory now. I can remember everything about my childhood but it's hard to remember where I put my kettle a few minutes before. It is funny but annoying'.

Lisie wanted to laugh but she didn't know how the old man would react. Moreover she didn't like the fact that ageing takes away precious things out of life. Age takes away beauty, hearing, eyesight, memory and finally the whole person fails to out run the course of age upon him. She felt compassion to the old man but his way of talking about his loss of memory in a funny way did flash a smile on her face.

'Coffee? For both'?

'Yes. Doruf, don't you want a coffee'?

The old man felt strange when Lisie spoke in English. He looked at Doruf as if he was seeking his permission but in fact he was observing Doruf. Doruf looked like a common Serbian youth and Lisie too. He knew it would be inappropriate to ask them why they talk in a foreign language. He didn't show them any sign that he was observing them. But he asked in Serbian,

'Where are you from?'

'Bari '. Lisie told him.

'What's your name'? The old man continued talking while he was preparing coffee.

'Lisie. What's your name'?

'Vilko'.

He served them coffee and two sweet breads. The old man decided to talk with Nick. He just wanted to know whether he could speak in Serbian.

'How are you young man? You seem really silent. Are you okay'?

Nick didn't know what to say. He understood the first few words. He knew how to say he was fine. But he didn't know what the rest of the old man's questions were. He remained confused for some time. Lisie knew it was her duty to help Nick. But before she made her move the old man looked at Lisie and asked her,

'He doesn't know Serbian, does he? Is he a foreigner?'

Lisie wasn't sure what to say. She took a few seconds to answer him. All the strength that she kept in herself from the moment Doruf started to behave like a new man was drained with that question. Even she wasn't sure what the answer was. She wanted to say 'no' but Nick told her several times that he was an English man, not a Serbian. She looked at Doruf's face with her frozen eyes. She told the old man,

'No. He is not a foreigner. But you are right he doesn't speak Serbian'.

Lisie turned around to hide her face from both of them. She pretended that she was searching Kaiser. Kaiser was near the river under tree shades, he was eating the light green fresh grass tops growing along the river side. Vilko understood his question wounded her mind. He felt sorry for the girl but he wasn't sure why. No one understands anyone at first glance. It is easier to judge immediately but it is impossible to be rightful to judge.

'Oh, have I hurt you somehow'? Vilko asked Lisie.

'No, it's not you. But I am hurt'. Lisie's words resembled a painful sob. Nick noticed Lisie. He asked her,

'What's wrong Lisie'?

'Nothing'.

'Tell me. Is there any problem'?

'Nothing Nick, I just want my Doruf back. I am an ordinary woman. I am failing to act stronger. I am afraid to lose him from my life'.

'You won't lose him Lisie. I deserve my wife just like how you deserve your fiancé. I can see how much you love Doruf. Your love won't be hopeless. I came here uninvited. I might leave here at any moment. Let's just hope the good at least till we meet your mother's friend'.

Vilko kept a little away from them. He wanted to give them enough privacy to discuss their own problems. Perhaps he felt guilty for asking that question. He questioned himself in his mind. He told himself that it was none of his problem in which language they spoke, it was nothing related to his life whether the young man was a foreigner or not. At last when Lisie was consoled Vilko approached them.

'I didn't mean to hurt you my child. I was just curious seeing you speak in a foreign language. But I have a suggestion to you dear. Don't keep your heart closed with your problems. You need to share it, at least with a stranger. Let me know your problem, I might be able to help you. I have seen life a lot more. And I say with my experience, help often comes from people we least expect'.

He was right. Lisie wanted somebody to tell her problem. She wanted to let it flow out of her mind. She felt an invincible conection with Vilko, a call from the depth of her mind wanted her to believe this old man. She couldn't hold it any longer. She burst into tears when she began to tell him everything from the night of the unusual snowfall. She told him how she lost her fiancé in the gap of an evening. She told him what Nick told about him when he came into Lisie's life through Doruf and about their journey. Nick remained silent. He understood what she was talking with the old man. As the wind was slowly passing them Lisie finished her words. It definitely was an unbelievable experience, Lisie expected him to be in disbelief. But instead of him she was left in disbelief seeing his reaction. Vilko looked at Nick and nodded his head as if he was seriously thinking about this problem. He didn't even realise that he was nodding his head. He kept looking at Nick with the realisation that he was looking at a Serbian young man's face. But at the same time he could see in those eyes an unknown individual staring back at him. Vilko said,

'I haven't heard anything similar in my entire life. If this man is right with his identity as Nick, I don't really know how to help you. But I know the person you are about to meet, I know Dorika. She would help you. She would solve this mystery'.

Lisie was happy to hear that. Out of happiness she held Nick's hand. She translated him what Vilko said,

'Nick, he said he knew Dorika before. He said she would help us for sure'.

'Really? How did he know her before'?

'Yes, yes. Let me ask him'. Lisie paused her words and asked Vilko. She spoke very quickly out of excitement.

'Vilko, how do you know her'?

The old man had a smile on his face. He gently laughed before he said,

'Well, we practiced certain rituals together. She continued the same way but I opted out. I had enough with magic and superstitions. I was one among them years before. Dorika, Dijana, Ana and I, we practiced to worship the supernatural. We were accused for witchcraft and expelled from our village. But we did no harm to anyone to be expelled. Nothing stopped Dorika, she was determined. The rest of us lived our lives how the society wanted us to live'.

Lisie remained speechless hearing the words of Vilko. Something shook her completely. She interrupted him,

'Vilko, Dorika is my mother's friend. My mother told me that she knew Dorika from childhood. She even visited our house several times'.

Vilko looked at her as Lisie still wasn't finished. After a pause she told him looking deep into his eyes,

'My mother is Dijana'.

'Oh! Oh my God', Vilko couldn't believe his ears. Lisie continued,

'But I didn't know my mother practiced witchcraft. She never gave me a hint. Could it be some other Dijana'?

'No, no, you have a similar face. Your lips, your eyes, you have facial features of Dijana'.

'Yes, I look like my mother'.

'I have no doubt. Your mother is our Dijana. I knew she went to the north. But I didn't know it was Bari '. He paused and held Lisie's hands. He continued,

'Ana went to the south with her uncle. But she didn't live longer. I still can't believe you are Dijana's daughter. Dorika informed me about your mother's death'.

He looked at Lisie with a sigh and told himself,

'It's just Vilko and Dorika remaining'.

Something Lisie didn't know

Lisie couldn't believe her mother used to practice witchery. But it was a truth she had to accept. Society has its own rigid unwritten laws, among them the most appealing one is about universality. It demands every member to behave in a similar way. It demands each to follow a similar life style. But there have always been rebels everywhere regardless of the time and place. Her mother was one among such rebels as she wanted to know more about the superstitions despite the barriers of society. She didn't blindly follow what others put forward. She wanted to know certain things on her own. But she was finally given the name 'witch girl' before she had to leave her place forever. They didn't push her or her family to move away, but none of them talked to her or her family like they used to. It was possibly because they were afraid. In a way Lisie proved herself one among such rebels like her mother when she decided to trust Nick. When others believed Doruf spoke nonsense she gave him a chance. She wanted to find the truth about Nick on her own despite denying him completely.

Lisie insisted on hearing more about her mother. Her questions deserved answers.

'But my mother didn't follow witchery after she moved away, neither of you did. Did my father know about this'?

'I don't know about that Lisie, I didn't even know she lived at Bari . But I know much about Dorika. She kept contact with me even after I stopped everything. I don't know why Dorika never told anything about Dijana till her death. I think Dijana wanted it to be so. I didn't ask her. It doesn't matter'.

Nick couldn't wait any longer. He interrupted them with his concerns. There was nothing wrong with that because he was also suffering. In fact he suffered more than Lisie. She lost only the mind of her fiancé Doruf but Nick lost everything, his wife, his world and even his identity. He wanted Lisie to translate his questions to Vilko. He told her,

'Lisie, I need to know something from him. Ask him what he thinks about my situation. What happened to me? Can he say how to go back to my place and time'?

Lisie asked Vilko about Nick's concerns. But she had no faith as he told her earlier that he stopped everything long ago. Vilko looked at Nick and spoke as Lisie translated for both of them.

'I am helpless Nick. I can't tell you what actually happened with you. But you should have your confidence. I told Lisie earlier that I never heard anything like your case. But it doesn't mean that you are trapped. I guess you know some people who can foresee future, we call them prophets. How do they do that? How do they see things that are supposed to happen in the long future? None of us have any idea about it. Some people are born with that gift to peep into the time. Do you know about Nostradamus, a French prophet'?

Nick replied,

'Yes, I have heard about him. But I don't know much'

'He lived in France about four hundred years before. But he was able to see more. He saw many more centuries ahead of him. He wrote in his prophesies what he saw. He wrote about many kings, many nations, many people and many warriors. All came true. Nostradamus was gifted with his power. You are almost like him, but instead of seeing time you travelled through it and reached here. You say you reached here from the future. But in our eyes Doruf has travelled into the future and he forgot himself. Both are correct and incorrect at the same time. Nostradamus did it purposefully. He knew what he was doing. But in your case even you don't know how you did it'.

'Can I go back? Is it possible'?

'If you could come here leaving your world it would be possible to go back as well. Your world doesn't exist in our view because it is future. But you are certain that it exists at this moment somewhere in time. You are certain that you have a wife, your own body and your own house. I cannot tell you how to regain them because I don't know. But I have a doubt. If your mind came along without your body, what happened to it? I think your body doesn't exist in your world'.

Lisie felt very difficult to explain Vilko's word to Nick. But she had to. They knew their way wouldn't be smooth. Nick was left demolished with Vilko's words. He asked panicking,

'What do you mean'?

Vilko wanted to be as gentle as he could to express his thoughts. But it wasn't a gentle thought. So he told Lisie directly,

'Tell him he is dead'.

Lisie didn't say a word. She stood confused. She felt that she was losing balance. She knew that could tear him apart. She told Vilko,

'You may be wrong Vilko. It can't be'.

'Lisie, he is either dead in his world or he is in a deep uninterrupted state of meditation. You should be truthful to him, tell him this'.

Lisie didn't tell in the way Vilko presented it. She told him,

'Nick, he said, you are in a deep meditation in your world'. And she continued,

'Or there is a mere possibility, it can't even be true. He says you may not be alive in your world anymore'.

'He says I am dead'?

'It's just a doubt'.

Nick looked powerless even to respond. He sat down on the dusty road. Lisie tried hard to strengthen him, to give him confidence to stand against his fate. She told him,

'Nick, it is not a final word. You cannot be dead'.

'Lisie I am not worried if I am dead. I am worried about Ann. I couldn't even tell her anything. She is there, alone in our house. She must be worried'.

He didn't cry, neither did his words tremble with sobs. He seemed emotionless and lost in a world where he was already lost.

'I wish to see her at least one more time'.

His despair was so palpable. Vilko understood his condition very well. He told him,

'Meet Dorika as early as you can. There isn't any use

spending time with me or anyone else. You need Dorika. She would at least be able to tell what happened to you'.

'Yes, you are right'.

Lisie called Kaiser. Kaiser was ready at her call for the rest of the journey. Lisie told Nick that they need to hurry to reach Avala before it gets too late in the night. Even though Nick was totally depressed while getting ready for the ride, he didn't forget to say good bye to Vilko. Lisie told Vilko,

'I am glad I met you here. I am happy to know something about my mother. We will visit you when we return from Avala'.

'I will pray for both of you. Don't waste time. It is still a long ride to reach her place'.

Lisie pulled Kaiser's harness and told him to move. He started galloping with a hiss. His hooves spattered dust in the direction of the wind and the tune of his steps drilled into the dry village road. It was an exhausting day. But clouds stayed against the tough sun throughout the day making it a lot easier for Lisie and Nick.

The Highlands of Avala

1914, Avala, Serbia

Lisie didn't need any signboard to say they were close to Avala when the roads began to be narrower. The landscape began to show its change with rocks and slops. Though it was getting darker Lisie decided to continue as she was sure Dorika's cottage was a few minutes away from them. The road finally began to circle around a hill like a snake trying to climb up a tree. Lisie was reminded of her mother's descriptions about Dorika's place. She could remember the circling road and hills. She told Nick,

'Nick, I think we reached her place. Dorika's house is very large if my mother was correct. She lives alone in a big house. It is big enough to be called a mansion. The house stands on a hill facing the cornfields down the hill. At the gate of her mansion two Chimney lamps would be hung. She does that for those who travel at night. Look carefully. Don't miss the house'.

As they were looking aside the path Kaiser stopped suddenly. He wasn't ready to move even a single step. He stopped as if somebody pulled his harness to stop. Lisie didn't know what happened to him, she asked him to move. But there wasn't any use,

'Kaiser, Kaiser, Go. It is just a little more'.

Kaiser responded to her words with a long hiss. Lisie understood from his hiss that he had something to tell. Lisie looked straight to the side where Kaiser was staring. It was dark, she could only see the trees and rocks standing still in the dark. But Lisie was sure that there was something bothering Kaiser.

'What's there Kaiser'? Lisie, asked him when she couldn't see anything there.

Nick tried to see what worried Kaiser. He looked watchfully with his hands placed above his eyebrows. Nick told Lisie in a whispering voice,

'Lisie, I see someone. Look among the trees on the left side. See, there's somebody with a horse. It is watching us'.

'I don't see'.

'Look, look to your left'.

Nick was right. Lisie saw what he explained. There was somebody on the left side of the road on a horse. The figure sitting on the horse talked in English in a female voice,

'You are looking for me. I am Dorika'.

Lisie and Nick remained speechless. They were amazed. But both of them were terrified. Dorika waited for them in the middle of the wood all by herself. They couldn't believe she sensed their arrival without any clue. Lisie touched Nick's hand. She wanted to hold tight on his hand to make herself stronger.

The figure on the horse continued,

'Why are you frightened, Lisie? You wanted to see me'?

As they remained silent, Dorika continued,

'No need to be worried. You travelled two days to meet me'.

Dorika was at least twenty feet away from them and it was very dark even to see each other. But Dorika went on talking as if she could see them very clear,

'You look extremely tired, both of you. Follow me. My house is just over there. You need to rest first. I have prepared your dinner. Let's go quickly'.

Nick had a smile on his face. He was convinced with Dorika's mystic powers. He was sure that he was with the right person. Kaiser followed Dorika. He didn't wait for Lisie's command. In the shallow light of the moon they found it difficult to see their way but they were ready to follow Dorika. At times of necessity even emperors blindly follow the narrower possibilities. Dorika kept talking to her visitors. But for some reason she didn't talk to Nick.

'Lisie, I know your friend doesn't speak our language. That is why I use English. Finally your father's English lessons turn out to be useful for you. Lisie, you don't even speak to me'.

Lisie became aware that her silence could mean absolute negligence. She knew she had to come out of her disbelief and talk with her.

'I'm listening to you, Dorika'. Lisie told her in Serbian. But Dorika wasn't happy with the answer as well as for using Serbian because Nick couldn't understand it. She told Lisie,

'Lisie, let's not put your friend in confusions. It is nice if we speak in English. He would be happy'.

Nick was happy to hear that. Dorika's consideration for him made Nick believe in her gentleness far beyond his faith in her exceptional powers. Dorika told them about her plan to visit her friend in the morning. And she told them that they would have to spend the morning by themselves as she would return from her friend only by the noon. But she had everything planned for her guests. She told them,

'Your breakfast would be ready for you on the table. You can eat it if you wake up early. But I think you should sleep till I come back from my friend. Both of you really need nice sleep'.

As they moved slowly following Dorika they finally reached the gates of a mansion. It looked a little old, but it was beautiful. The gate wasn't closed and as Lisie told earlier there were two Chimney lamps hung on both sides of the gate. As they walked into the gates they could smell the aroma of rose flowers. It insisted their eyes to look at Dorika's garden. In the dim light of the moon and chimney lamps they saw a lot of rose flowers enjoying themselves the solemnity of the night. Dorika took them into her wonderful house. She served them a delicious dinner. Lisie and Nick couldn't enjoy their meal even though they were very hungry and tired. They wanted to tell her their problem. Dorika already knew it. But she waited for Lisie and Nick to reveal it.

'Dorika, I need a help'. Lisie slowly untied the mysteries about Nick and Doruf. She wanted to tell her how Doruf became Nick. But Dorika interrupted her.

'Lisie, you have brought an unusual question to me. I know your problem, I know why you travelled all the way from Bari to me in two days. I need to see into him. It will take time, may be more than an hour to get all your answers. We don't have to hurry, we can do it tomorrow'.

But Nick wasn't ready to wait anymore. He was thriving to know what happened to him. More than that he wanted to make sure what happened to Andria. He looked at Lisie. She

121

knew what was in his mind, so she told Dorika,

'Can we do it now? We hurried to you to know everything as early as we could'.

'Yes, I don't have any problem. I thought it is better for you to rest now'.

'He won't sleep tonight Dorika. He really wants to know about himself'. Lisie continued,

'I wouldn't rest peacefully if I keep thinking about Doruf'.

'It's okay Lisie. Finish your meal. I will prepare myself for the ritual. Don't come into the room till I say, it's supposed to be a secret'.

As they finished their dinner they had to wait for Dorika's call. She kept her room closed for a long time. Lisie and Nick could hear some chants from the room. But they couldn't understand anything as it was so feeble. Lisie and Nick waited patiently. The hearth was still burning. Rattling sound of the burning charcoal filled an uncertainty into the thoughts of Nick and Lisie. Finally Dorika opened the door she said,

'It's ready, come sit with me'.

Dorika the Gypsy woman

1914, Avala, Serbia

Dorika took them both into her special room where she practice study and do experiments with the art of witchcraft, other rituals and her visions into the future. Lisie and Nick sat together opposite to Dorika. Between them Dorika kept a white piece of cloth. Dorika kept looking at Nick's face and at the white piece of cloth. She touched above the cloth and moved her fingers as if she was drawing some lines over it. A gentle smile appeared on her face as she saw something very interesting.

Dorika looked at Nick and asked him,

'What's your name'?

Nick didn't have a good answer to give. He didn't really know who he was. He was confused, but he said,

'Nick'

'Are you Nick, or do you have something else to say?', Dorika had a gentle smile on her face.

'I'm Nick, my mind is still Nick. But I am not in my body; I'm in Lisie's fiancé's body. He was called Doruf. I am in his body but my life and mind belong to Nick.'

'I know you had a strange story to tell, you were living in an English city far away with your lovely wife Andria. You moved to a new house and spent one night there, that's what you remember'

Nick was in absolute disbelief, he looked into her eyes. He felt scared to be there but he knew he finally reached somewhere where all his questions could be answered. He moved his head in approval.

'Nick, did you see those rose flowers in my garden?'

'Yes'

'I call each flower different names. When one falls some

other blooms and I give them new different names. This week I've a lot of them, but last week they were all buds preparing to bloom. For the next week I've some other buds, they will take time and I must wait. I must wait for one flower to fall and the other to bloom. You are the same, Nick. You are like one flower in my garden with your name. One day, you'll fall and another will bloom in your place with a different name. But when we think, they're all the same if we don't name them. Today's flower, tomorrow's flower and yesterday's flower, but they're all flowers. It is we who name them, it's time that separates them from the plant and brings death and birth. It is time that brings wrinkles on their soft petals, just like it brings wrinkles on our skin'.

She looked at Nick just to see whether he was following her. He answered her,

'I understand'.

'So, Nick. Don't worry with your names. I'll tell you some other secrets about your life. Some secrets you must know because you are special. Dorika looked at Lisie and continued to Nick,

'Nick, before you were Nick do you know who were you?'

Nick didn't have any idea about his own path till he reached Nick, he remained silent. He shook his head,

'You were a monk in a Buddhist monastery in India, your name was Prahlad. In that lifetime you travelled along India and Ceylon. You went to China crossing the Himalayas. Prahlad's lifetime was sixty years long. Prahlad died in India in a monastery at peace'.

She paused for a while and looked into Nick's eyes for a while as if she was seeking something from them. Then she continued,

'It was before Prahlad you were Doruf and had a life here in Serbia with Lisie. You have travelled two generations in reverse from our future to us, to Lisie. If you have travelled from future to Lisie, you might have something unfinished here and your energy wanted you to do it. Your travel from future is a proof of the inexistence of Lisie, me, you and even the time itself. It is not us that exists, it is our energy that exists. Our life is like a drama, filled with different characters and stages written on a paper. The drama doesn't exist, but its writer does. Time doesn't exist, even time is pre-written like our lives. You're not here Nick, you still are with your wife in 2014 and that's the reason your body doesn't came along with you. It's your energy that travelled because of some strange coincidences in 2014. I can see your body, the body of Nick in a hospital bed. He's unconscious and his energy is here with all the memories of Nick in Doruf's body'.

Lisie sat hearing all these in disbelief but very patient and attentive. And Dorika continued,

'Your past is even more interesting. Before you became Doruf, you were a blind man in Arabia, but you were very rich. You had many slaves. You did so many cruelties in that lifetime than in any other lifetimes you had. You had used many girls for your sexual pleasure in that blind life and had

126

them killed when you were pleased. But your death was a pay off, you were lost in the desert one night when your trained camel died on your way home. You walked along the desert all night in cold and in the next day you died in the heat of the desert'.

She continued,

'Before that, you were a Tribal king in an island that is no more on this planet. You were called, Paghu; Paghu the great king. You had fourteen wives in that life but not even one child. Paghu failed to keep his royal line. He realised his ferocious battles and victories over other islanders were useless without a child of his own. But he wasn't ready to be a forgotten king. He ordered all craftsmen among his islands to make statues of himself in his royal costume. Many hands worked days and nights producing statues of their king. All those statues were fixed among the islands he ruled. All the islands he was proud for keeping under control is unknown for mankind. Everything he made with furious battles and his legendary life was snatched from him by a furious chain of waves. It didn't take even a couple of minutes to wipe out everything from the surface of the earth. He is forgotten indeed'.

Dorika was calm. But an invisible energy was surrounding her while she was going deep into the life cycles of Nick, Prahlad, Doruf, Blind man and Paghu the king. She looked even deeper into their lives. She continued,

'Before Paghu, you were a slave in Egypt. You had a tough life. But you finally found peace in that lifetime when you were loved by a young woman. She was the younger daughter of a wealthy man. You escaped from Egypt with the girl and lived four years with her. Later you were captured and imprisoned. They beheaded you for loving her. They accused you for kidnapping her'.

'Before the life of a slave, you were a corn seed that didn't germinate because you were eaten by a child. Before being a corn seed you were an alga that grew on a rock in the beaches of Scotland. That was your first life on Earth'.

Lisie and Nick remained silent when Dorika kept on going back into the cycle of life.

'Before being an alga you were shapeless, you were a gas molecule in the Sun. You were a part of the Sun'.

Dorika looked at Nick with a pleasant smile, she told him.

'Now, Nick don't you want to know your future? Your life after Nick?'

'Yes, but don't tell about my death when I am Nick, don't tell anything about my life as Nick. I want to live free without any knowledge'.

'Yes, I will tell you the rest. After your life being Nick, you will be born as the prince of England and you will be crowned at a very young age as the King of England. And in the next birth, you will be working in the same palace as a garden keeper and you will do your job very well. After that, you will become a shellfish. You will live that life near the beaches of Ecuador. And before returning back to the Sun to be a shapeless part of it, you will live the life of an alga one more time, deep under the ocean somewhere in the Pacific'

Lisie and Nick remained silent but curious about the mysteries of this universe and the cycles of life. It was then Dorika asked him one question,

'Nick, now tell me who are you? Are you the King of England, Garden keeper, Nick, Prahlad, Doruf, The blind man, Paghu the King, Slave in Egypt or the alga or the sea shell? Who are you?'

'I don't know. But I am all of them. Name makes no meaning to me'.

Dorika told him one thing to get him out of the shock of facing reality.

'Nick, you are special. You are Doruf and Nick too. It's just your energy that was carried back to the time by something along with the memories you had. Everything happens for a reason, it is pre-planned in the life of Nick to travel through time, it is pre-planned in the life of Andria to wait for you. You are Doruf as well, time is just a feeling, you will see your Andria at the right time but you have to wait. We have to wait for one flower to fall and the other to bloom. The buds are meant to be buds and flowers are meant to be flowers and then something else, it is the cycle of lives'

Dorika continued,

'You can earn only one thing out of your life, that's not wealth but love. Love your life, whatever it is. Love this moment of your feeling of time, there is only one thing we can enjoy in our life, this moment. We can't hold it, we can only enjoy. Lisie is your love, love her and don't hesitate. Andria is there, she loves Nick and Doruf is here and Doruf can love Lisie without any fear of regret. We never have to complain about our life, it is as it is meant to be'.

Three Circles of the universe

1914, Avala, Serbia

Mysteries of one's own lives in the course of the universe remained always a puzzle for everyone except Nick. He understood his love for himself and for his identity were all a pointless affection. He sensed how futile was it rejecting Lisie's love but still his humane instincts befell himself with the thoughts of Andria. He was still worried about the life he had with Andria. He still didn't understand how he could travel from one century to another. It was not just into his previous life but beyond his previous life that was lived in India as a monk in a monastery. He asked himself in wonder and asked Dorika to give him an answer about its possibility,

'Tell me how I travelled from my time to yours. How can you be alive? All of you are supposed to be dead. Time has passed'.

'Nick, remember what I told you, it's just your energy that has travelled not you. You were there in the past, you are here in present and you will be there in future too, but in different names and shapes. That's pre-written. Time is like a long ribbon that is stretched across the universe and all our life cycles are marked on it, once you learn to bend the ribbon you will see what is written there before or after your position, because you see it from a different angle. In your case, the ribbon of time is bent by someone and Nick's place in the ribbon is somehow tied together with Doruf's. Simply saying, Nick is in contact with Doruf. Past, present or future, nothing exists. Time is just a perception, a feeling that could be felt only for the living beings as when we move over the same ribbon. What is written in the life of Doruf will be the same and what is for Nick has no strange story to tell, if Nick is misplaced by accident in time he will be placed properly, that's for sure. But we don't know how long it would take. Time is constant; it is the pages in the story of creation, whatever is written would be the same'.

Lisie was puzzled she didn't hesitate to clarify everything, she wanted to make sure that she gets her Doruf back and helps her new love to reach his own love that was lost in time. She asked Dorika,

'Dorika, what does that mean? What's written will remain the same. What do you mean?'

'Simple, Lisie. Doruf's destiny will follow him, it won't change. Your destiny and mine, everyone is the same, we don't follow our destiny, destiny follows us'

Nothing changed Nick's mind as Andria was deeply imprinted in him. He looked at Dorika with his eyes of helplessness. He told her,

'What you say might be right, but my heart belongs to the world where I lived. I love Andria'.

'Nick, you should understand that your body that was called 'Nick' is struggling for its survival in the future', Dorika continued, 'You are not Nick, you are Doruf. It is Doruf's life you are in. It is just the memories of Nick that bothers you. You were not only Nick, you were Prahlad, you were the Blind man and Paghu who had fourteen wives. You know you will ascend the crown of England but you don't miss it, you don't feel the pain of dying in the desert boiling under the sun. Andria is the same, she is a different story, a different world that doesn't deserve Doruf's feelings. I'm not telling you to forget her but I'm asking you to wait for one flower to fall and the other to bloom, buds are meant to be buds without names. They don't deserve names till they are bloomed'.

Truth sometimes would be hard but they are what they are. Nick's mind in Doruf was ready to accept the existence of Doruf, Nick told himself that there wasn't the need of keeping him worried in this world. He looked at Lisie with a smile; it wasn't just a smile if Lisie was able to recognize its essence. She was happy to see him smile, she knew he was solving all the problems that tormented his mind. Dorika took her hands off from the magic bowl and asked Nick,

'Nick, there's one thing you should do before the morning brings the rays of sun and another to be done now. But you should do it with all your heart and love, with clear understanding that you are both Nick and Doruf'

'What are they, what should I do?'

'For now you shall kiss Lisie. Then you shall spent a night with her and give her your love'

Lisie and Nick looked at each other. Lisie felt embarrassed, within the depth of her mind her Doruf was a new man, a stranger. Nick felt uncomfortable; he didn't want to do it. But as strong as he was longing for Andria there was a current of love beyond his conscious mind that wanted to join with Lisie and her unconditional love. It was only Lisie who stood with him in this new world, it was only Lisie who gave her faith on his words and it was she who gave him the warmth of love when he needed it the most. Nick was ready to accept that he was completely in love with Lisie. He looked into Lisie's eyes, she found it very difficult to look at him. But in each glance she gave him, he could see what she wanted to hide as the rays of her love emitted without her permission. Nick asked her,

'Shall I?'

Lisie didn't say anything but she closed her eyes to escape from his look that made her more embarrassed. She moved her face closer to him with her eyes closed. Nick tasted her love without any fear of regret. He tasted it till he understood that the one thing he wouldn't want to lose in the lifetime of Doruf is Lisie's love.

'I love you both', Lisie whispered.

Dorika interrupted them with her soft voice and smile.

'Do you know the three circles of the universe which keep the balance of everything? Every book say the same, every religion in the world talk about this in their own different ways. They're the circle of life, time and the circle of existence'.

Lisie and Nick told her that they never heard about it. As they were patient to Dorika's words she explained to them what were the three circles and what did they do for the balance of the universe. She began,

'As it is said, in the beginning there was nothing in this universe but an omnipresent void. The void was the supreme element of the endless universe. It was then, out of the void the first creation was made, the heavens and the earth. They were separated from the void with a circle; the first circle of creation. They were the first things that existed in the whole universe and thus this circle is named 'the circle of existence'. And then within this circle another creation was made, they were days and nights and it was because of the nights and days the concept of time began. This creation was separated from the first creations with another circle and it is known as 'the circle of time'. Within the circle of time a very minor creation was made, life. The life was separated from the circle of time with another circle and it became the circle of life'.

Dorika continued,

'Living beings are vulnerable to time, time would age them, decay them and vanish them. It is because the circle of life is subjected within the circle of time. But time would never be influenced by life as the life remained smaller and surrounded by the time. But time is not supreme. Beyond its circle there was the circle of existence to surround it with the heavens and the earth and all other planets and stars. They have no feelings of time, they revolve around the time while time revolve around the lives. Days and nights are just the shadow magic of the planets and stars and thus they remained untouched by the time. But still, the circle of existence was not the supreme because around the circle of existence the omnipresent void stood still giving balance to the existence, time and lives. The void stood supreme by being empty. It is up to the time to decay the lives, up to the existence to keep time an illusion and up to the void emptiness to carry the existing inside.'

Lisie and Nick sat speechless, they thought about it. Dorika sounded right with each word she said. Nick couldn't resist his temptation and tongue,

'You are right, that's how everything is balanced.'

'Yes, Nick. I told you this because you feel you are fooled by time. But time doesn't exist, it is just like us, doing its part of the game but in fact doing nothing. It is just an energy everywhere called with different names.'

She stood up from her chair. She gave her hands to Lisie and Nick to help them stand up. She told them,

'Come with me, you must be tired. You can use the first room after the stairs. It is the best for guests'.

A Special Night

Dorika gave them both some mead that's been preserved for many years in the basement of her house. Dorika asked them to sleep comfortably. She arranged their room, gave them the best woollen blankets she had and put a bottle of water on the wooden table. It was really late in the night, but before going to bed it was Dorika's routine to walk up to the valleys. She couldn't resist her heart's longing to listen to the mountain breeze and the music of the night. Dorika told them as she was leaving their room,

'I am going out for a walk. Sleep well. And remember, I will go to my friend in the morning. I will come back by the afternoon. Your breakfast will be ready on the dining table. I cannot change my plan. Lisie, be comfortable here, my house is all yours'.

Lisie smiled politely. But Nick wanted to know something else. He asked,

'Dorika, where are you going now'?

'Just up to the valleys. It's very calming there'.

'Do you want to go alone or can we come along with you'?

Dorika smiled at him. She said,

'It's okay Nick, I can go alone. But if you want to come, you are most welcome'.

Nick and Lisie were tired with their travel but they decided to go out with Dorika. The night was beautiful with its sky filled with stars. And a light wind carried with it the moisture of the frozen mountain tops. Highlands and valleys were the beauty of Dorika's place. A melancholic music of nightingales echoed in the valleys. They sat on a flat rock from there they could see the wide valley and the mountains. She told her guests to listen to the music of the nightingales. She listened to its tune. She said,

'If you keep your eyes closed you can hear more. Your hearing will show you what your eyes failed to see. Sometimes it is better to close our eyes and follow our hearing'.

The cold mountain breeze rushed upon them through the tall black pines. But they were comfortable in their fur clothes. Dorika opened her eyes after some time like a monk from a peaceful meditation. Lisie and Nick still had their eyes closed when Dorika told them,

'Hear the echoes of the nightingale. It is confusing us with the real music. It is hard to find the real music and its echoes. But they all seem beautiful like the other, don't they?'

Nick said, 'Yes, they are similar, melodic'.

'Aren't we like the echoes of the music? We begin our life here, then we echo in the world at different places in different forms. We cannot say the echoes aren't real. Because we hear them, and we feel them just like how we felt the real music. So they are as real as the music itself. Our lives are the same. In all our births our lives are beautiful in one way or the other. It doesn't matter how loud or feeble we echo'.

Nick definitely missed his wife Andria. But he was ready to accept it. He could imagine how difficult it would be for Andria to handle that situation. Dorika's promise that he would meet Andria again gave him the strength to be happy in Doruf's world. He knew his responsibility for Lisie. He was Doruf, destined to love Lisie. Nick was ready to love her with the realisation that Lisie was once his lover. Nick broke the silence, he told his thoughts aloud to Lisie and Dorika,

'I must say something. I was so proud about my country, I mean Britain. I was so proud to tell anyone that I belonged to the United Kingdom. But, here I am sitting with you as one of you. How futile is the feeling of patriotism? How futile is it to be proud of any country'.

Dorika wasn't just a witchcraft practitioner. She knew enough politics to talk about the world.

'You are right, look at the world. Ottomans, Germans, Austria- Hungary, France, Italy, Russia all are in trouble. It makes no sense to me. There must be some way to avoid problems. No one wants it. It is changing so quickly. Each one of them is busy filling their armoury. Anything can happen at any time'.

Nick wanted to tell her about the war that would break out in the year 1914. He wanted to tell her that it would start from the soil of Serbia. But he didn't want to tell her about the deadly war when Lisie was listening. He didn't want to frighten her. But he knew Dorika was aware of it. If Dorika was able to see his life in the future as the prince of England, as a garden keeper, as a shellfish, he was sure that she could see what would happen to her own country in the near future.

'Let's go back, its colder than I thought. You might fall sick', Dorika warned them about the mountain breeze.

'This wind is not familiar for you. It is extremely cold and your body needs time to find the balance with the variations of air-pressure. So let's just go back and get some sleep'.

They walked back to the house. At that exact time Kaiser made his new friend. It was Dorika's horse. He was also dark black like Kaiser. He had splendid food at Dorika's barn. That was enough to rejuvenate his mind and body from a tiring hundred miles long journey. Lisie and Nick wanted to sleep. They couldn't resist their tiredness anymore as they reached the house they hurried to the room where Dorika arranged their bed. Lisie didn't even realise that she fell asleep the moment she touched the bed. Nick was laid beside Lisie on the same bed. He looked at her face; he could see it on her face how tired she actually was. Sunlight slightly burnt her skin and under her eyes a light dark shade showed up. She took deep breaths as if she desperately needed more air. Nick couldn't take his eyes off her face; he felt that he was looking at the face of Andria. His mind made him believe that time, death, life or even his own existence didn't matter while watching her. He knew she trusted his words when others called him mad, she wiped his tears when others thought it meant nothing. It was all because of her love. She

140

loved him. She loved her fiancé Doruf who's none other than Nick himself. She took him all the way without thinking about any possible hazard. He finally merged himself into the reality that she was his soul mate at a forgotten time. Nick wanted to tell her something, so he decided to call her. He gently called her name,

'Lisie'

But she was so tired. Her tiredness put her in a deep sleep with some dreams. Whatever she saw in her dream made her smile in her sleep. Nick touched her hand. He took her palm and quietly placed it over his chest without disturbing her sleep. He closed his eyes with a sigh. His left hand was lightly holding her palm to his chest, perhaps he wanted to make sure it was there all night long. They slept peacefully.

Love blooms

Lisie and Nick didn't notice the sunlight out in the garden, but it was already ten in the morning. Dorika wasn't home as she told them last night. She went to meet her friend. It was perhaps Kaiser who woke Lisie up from her sleep. He was calling out for Lisie when he couldn't see her even when the morning sun hit him with its rays. Lisie finally had to get up from the bed to say hello to Kaiser. She wanted to let him know that she didn't leave him behind. But as she woke up she noticed something unusual. It was the change in Nick; she could see how close he laid beside her. He never did that from the moment they started their journey. Lisie wanted to kiss him on his check. There was nothing wrong with that as he was in fact her fiancé. She kissed him on his cheek with a fear in her mind about his reaction. She tried not to wake him up. So her kiss was as soft as a flower's petal. She whispered in his ears in Serbian,

'Volim te'.

She didn't want to leave him. But Kaiser wasn't ready to calm down. As Lisie was about to leave the room Nick woke up from his sleep. He was still sleepy and it made a bit difficult for Lisie to understand what he asked her,

'Lisie, was it Serbian'?

As Lisie couldn't hear him properly she stopped there and

looked at his face. She asked him,

'What'?

'Was it Serbian? You said something when you kissed my cheeks'.

Lisie didn't say anything for a few seconds. But after a pause she told him,

'Yes'.

'Was it 'I love you'?

'Yes', she admitted hiding her shyness and fear.

'How did you say that'?

'Volim te'. She continued, 'It is, Volim te, means I love you'.

'Oh, okay'. He pushed off the quilt off his body and sat on the bed. He asked her,

'Where are you going Lisie'?

'Just want to see Kaiser, he is worried'.

'Okay, okay'. 'Carry on Lisie'.

Lisie smiled at him as she walked out of the room. Nick remained on the bed but he wanted to say something to Lisie. A gentle smile bloomed on his face. He called Lisie a little louder,

'Lisie'.

She didn't know why he called her. She wasn't sure what happened to him. Perhaps her worries about him made her think that something was wrong. She ran back into the room. As she reached the door, she saw him smiling at her. She didn't know what made him smile. She asked him,

'What happened? You scared me'.

'Volim te'.

Lisie smiled at him. Her eyes became brighter but a drop of tear flowed over her cheek. She felt in her heart that she got her Doruf back. Nick told her again,

'Volim te'.

Lisie replied him with tears on her face,

'Volim te, volim te'.

She embraced him with all her love. She cried for a few minutes. It was not merely some tears, it was tears of joy. Nick didn't feel any regret for welcoming Lisie into his mind. He knew he had to accept the truth that he was in a different time where his love was Lisie. He knew he was Doruf once in his past and he knew he came back from his own time to Lisie's time. He didn't know what else to do in their world, he felt loving Lisie was his only duty. He didn't know anything else in his own forgotten past indeed.

Lisie kept calling him Doruf again and again as if she was making herself believe that she got him back. Nick held her close to him, because by then he had completely accepted himself as Doruf even though he still didn't remember anything about Doruf. He still couldn't speak Serbian; he didn't remember being called Doruf. But he simply knew that he was Doruf. Lisie asked him,

'Are you my Doruf now'?

Nick didn't have to think anymore.

'I am. I am Doruf', he said.

Lisie laughed with happiness but her eyes were still pouring tears over her cheeks. Nick told her with a little bit of hesitation. He was afraid he would spoil all her happiness with his words. So he told her in broken sentences,

'But, Lisie.... I.... I don't remember anything'.

Lisie knew what kind of thoughts confronted his mind. She smiled at him and told him.

'It's okay Doruf. It's okay. I am here to believe you. We know what happened. Don't worry about that'.

'I still can't speak Serbian. I don't remember even my parents here. What would you tell others when they find out that I don't speak your language anymore? What would you tell them when they find out that I don't remember any of them including my family and yours? And I miss Andria who lives in another time as my wife.'

'I know you miss her. I can't complain about that. Why would I Doruf? If Doruf is Nick there, it might be me who became Andria. I would believe it in that way. I may be wrong, but I would believe it. She is me'.

Then Lisie told him,

'Doruf, I don't mind whether you remember me or not. Don't worry even if you can't remember anything. We will begin everything from zero. I will be with you. Do you believe me'?

She looked into his eyes when she asked him that. He had a predictable answer to give her. He said,

'I trust you Lisie. I know you will be with me here'.

'Yes, I will be'. She was stern. It was clear in her words that she would go beyond all limitations for him'. She continued,

'Don't worry about facing our people. Tell them what happened. Let who believes you believe and others disbelieve. You have nothing to prove others but only yourself. You know who you are'.

Lisie's words gave him the strength that he had someone to hold on. That was all he wanted in his own world that became unknown to him. He looked at her. His eyes were filled with gratitude. But he was reminded of Kaiser. He told Lisie,

'Lisie, aren't going to see Kaiser'?

'Oh, yes. I forgot he was calling me'.

Lisie went out to Kaiser. He was calmed when he saw Lisie. She spent some time with him. She didn't forget to fondle his neck and cuddle him in the middle of her happiness. She saw there was enough food for him in the barn. Dorika arranged it for him before she left to meet her friend. Lisie went back to Dorika's house to check whether Dorika prepared food for them. She knew she didn't have to because Dorika had already pleased them with her hospitality. Lisie wanted to serve breakfast for her Doruf. On that morning Lisie and Doruf sat together and enjoyed their breakfast at Dorika's house. They went out with Kaiser for a short ride through the village roads and valleys. Avala was completely different to their eyes in the morning. All those dark woods they saw in the night that caused them fear seemed very beautiful in the daylight. And from the valleys they could see Dorika's house very clearly as it was massive enough. They couldn't believe that they failed to spot such a gigantic house. Lisie and Nick returned to Dorika's house by the afternoon with the expectation that Dorika would be home by then. They were absolutely right, she had returned a little earlier as she didn't want Lisie and her fiancé to be lonely at her place. Dorika was waiting for them impatient. She had a bad news to tell. It was nothing about them, but it in fact was a threat even for them. Dorika couldn't welcome them with a smile as she was concerned about some serious matter. She told them,

'It's going to be chaos soon. It's going to be horrible from now on'.

Lisie and Nick had no clue about it. They were worried whether they made some mistake. Lisie asked her in disbelief,

'What happened, Dorika? Did we do something wrong'?

Dorika looked at them. She handed over a newspaper to them saying,

'It's not your mistake. It's not our mistake but we are all under trouble now'.

Lisie went through the articles. She didn't have to go through the newspaper a lot. Her eyes were stuck on the headlines of the first page. Her face told Nick that there was something terribly wrong. As Lisie kept reading the news Nick asked her,

'What's wrong Lisie?'

'Oh, Doruf it's a big problem'.

Fear

Lisie read and explained the news to her new Doruf.

'It's about a murder, an assassination. Archduke of Austro-Hungary is shot dead by someone. It is written that Austro-Hungarian Empire says that the assassin is supported by Serbia. Archduke's wife is also killed. The culprit is arrested. He tried to shoot himself after killing Archduke but they captured him alive. Austrians are absolutely provoked. The newspaper says that they might declare a war on Serbia'.

Nick looked at her. He was reminded of the First World War. He couldn't believe his ears even though he was expecting the fury of the war upon Lisie and her people. He couldn't remember the month of World War's beginning from the moment he started to worry about Lisie and all those innocent people living there. But now he knew what would happen. He was interested in history, particularly in the area of World Wars. He reminded himself that exactly one month after the assassination took place Austria declared war on Serbia. He wanted to tell Lisie that it would happen. He wanted to tell her to get away from her country without wasting anytime in Serbia. He knew it wasn't safe in the whole Europe. It wasn't safe especially in Belgrade where the war literally started. He was truly in trouble. He didn't know whether he should tell her everything about the war or keep himself silent. Because he knew the truth would definitely destruct her. He didn't want to let her live in terror. He looked at Dorika helplessly. Dorika shook her head slowly as if she wanted to warn him not to tell anything about the war. Nick knew she could never be wrong, so he obeyed her. He didn't tell Lisie anything.

'Doruf, we need to go home. I want to see my family. I should be with them'.

Lisie was already consumed with fear. She forgot her word that she would speak in English at Nick's presence. She told Dorika in Serbian,

'Dorika, I wanted to stay with you for some days. But I can't stay here. I must go back. My father is there, my sisters are there'.

'Lisie, nothing will happen. Believe my words. It is politics. They can't do anything so quickly. Even if they want to fight, they won't attack all of a sudden. If you want to go back, you can start tomorrow. Look, it's already afternoon. You can't reach anywhere before night and you can't travel in the night. So listen to my words, you can go back tomorrow morning'.

Lisie wasn't pleased with Dorika's idea. But she couldn't say no. She had to accept Dorika.

'Dorika, would it be okay? Are you sure that they are safe

there'?

Dorika made her believe that nothing would happen to her family back in Belgrade. In fact Dorika was truthful, because they were all safe for the next thirty days. The war was supposed to break out on the 28th of July 1914 if Nick was right. As he was aware, exactly one month after the assassination took place the war was declared against Serbia. The date of the news paper was 29th of June 1914. That meant they had enough time to reach Belgrade safe. Nick didn't feel comfortable for hiding it from Lisie. He wanted to tell her, he wanted to take her away to somewhere where she would be safe. He knew they could go somewhere away from the eyes of Army. He knew Belgrade wasn't safe as it was easier for Austrian military to reach. He wanted to take her to places far away from the eyes of military. Mountain peaks or caves, it didn't matter he just wanted to save her. But still he didn't tell her because Dorika told him not to. Nick wanted to talk about it with Dorika without Lisie's attention. He waited for that moment.

When they ate lunch he tried to talk about it with Dorika but he couldn't as Lisie was beside him. When Dorika was in her garden Nick attempted it again, but Lisie followed him. Finally when Lisie went into the barn to check on Kaiser Nick approached Dorika. He asked her,

'Dorika, can I tell her about the war? I can't hide it from her. It's not safe there. That place is going to be sacked'.

'I know. But don't tell her'.

'Why? I can take her somewhere away from danger. War doesn't harm people who are away from military engagement. Just tell them to leave their place. Tell to stay away'.

'How long would you take her away from her death'?

'I don't really understand you, Dorika'.

'Nick, you are aware of it just because you happened to live in the so called future. She didn't. She lives like others without any knowledge about very next moment. Belgrade will be attacked. Thousands will die very soon. You can't help them neither can I'.

Dorika took his hand. She told him in secret,

'You can't help her get away from her destiny. If her destiny wants her to die in the war no one can help her. It will hunt her down, no matter how far you take her away. It is the same in our case too, you and me. Are you afraid of death? What actually is it Nick? You know it better than me. You are already in a dead world, don't you think so? You are already in a dead world even in your own time. It is just a matter of going through the pages of our own different roles. One ends somewhere and the other begins to follow the same path. I won't tell you to run away from Belgrade. There is no point even if you run away. I can clearly see that'.

'But Dorika, I still can't let her be in trouble. I want her to be happy'.

She could see how much he cared for Lisie's safety. She told him,

'Nick, there is only one thing you can do for her. Be her Doruf, love her. Marry her. Give yourself. That would make her happy. Happiness is not for ever for a long time. Nobody manages to keep their happiness till the end of their lives. It is made instantly and felt instantly. It is not about how long you can feel happiness but how much happiness you can feel. So give her in abundance. We are not certain of our lives, so love unconditionally and make happiness in abundance. Fear not'.

Nick wasn't in a state to accept everything she told. Dorika knew it. She continued,

'It's not easy, I know. But think about it Nick. What is the point in terrifying Lisie? Go back to Belgrade in the morning. Marry her before the war tarnishes our lives. Perhaps it could be the last present you can give Lisie before travelling back to Andria in 2014. Nick, time has brought you back to fulfil something you couldn't do a century before. These are beyond our imagination, knowledge and reach. All of us are unaware why we live here. It is our destiny to blindly follow certain elements that revolve around our life'.

Nick had to believe her words. There was nothing else he could tell himself. He turned around as he was failing to hold his tears. His eyes were gazed at the roses in the garden. At the other side of the garden, he could see Lisie fondling Kaiser. He felt sorry for Lisie as she was completely unaware of the trauma approaching her life. He felt sorry for the children he saw waving at him innocently on his way to Niš.

He knew their life was at the verge of a dramatic turn. A single drop of tear dripped from his eyes to the bare ground. Dorika knew his feelings. She knew how much he felt guilty for hiding it from those innocent villagers. She asked him,

'Why do you keep thinking about saving them? Are you not going to save yourself'?

'No, I don't care about me. I know I have a place to go. This is not meant for me, I am supposed to be somewhere else'.

'It is the same for them, even for me'. Dorika countined,

'They all have similar promised places to go like you think you have England. And they all have people to be with like you have Andria after this life. But there is a difference between you and them. They are not aware of it but you are. I told you before that time don't exist in the eyes of our creator. Our feeling that we are confined in our world is just a false impression. In reality we are everywhere regardless of the time and regardless of our shape. We are all part of something that is unknown to us. Look at these flowers, look at the soil that nourish its plant, think of the worms living underneath, think of water that helps both of them to stay alive, think about the bees visiting this garden, birds who sing among these valleys, clouds above these mountains that brings rain. Think about you, think about Lisie and Kaiser, nothing is permanent, none is real. All is part of one single unknown entity. That means you are not different from anything else you see. When you realise that you are part of that one single entity you will understand your identity, your surroundings and even time is worthless.

Dorika stopped for some time giving Nick enough time to think about her words. And she continued,

'If you are aware of this, you won't bother about your identity, you won't bother about your nationality, and you won't bother about following any religion or God. You won't bother about death. You will see yourself everywhere'.

Nick knew Dorika was right. He was aware of it perhaps better than anyone else. He accidentally happened to travel from his life into his own previous life. Being alive in his own past dead life proved him nothing actually ended neither began. It proved him that time is just a highly sensitive feeling between existence and pseudo existence. He informed his willingness to obey her by saying,

'Of course, you are right. I should let her be happy. I should be her fiancé. I should live here like them without knowing how coarsely the world would fight each other. I should at least act like them'.

'Careful, Lisie is coming', she warned Nick. Without knowing what they were nattering about Lisie joined them with a smile on her face. She asked Nick,

'Doruf, are we going in the morning'?

'Yes', he continued, 'Dorika was saying that we should marry soon'.

Lisie was surprised and confused hearing it on the spur of the moment. She wanted to smile showing her happiness and agreement but she couldn't smile. She rather asked Dorika,

'Why so quickly'?

Dorika had to tell her something without letting her anticipate anything. She intervened,

'It is just the right time Lisie. Doruf needs you now. It would make things a lot easier for him in his self recovery'.

Dorika knew she wouldn't question anymore as she proposed marriage as a healing for Doruf. Lisie was more than happy to do anything for the sake of Doruf. She said,

'It is decided to be on the 2nd of August. Can't we wait?'

'No, no. Not so long', Dorika told her after calculating in her mind that the war would have already started by then. But she deliberately told some other excuses to make it a little earlier.

'It would be so much better if you both start living together at the earliest. Tell your father to make arrangements'.

'I don't know, he wouldn't like to rush'.

'No one would like it Lisie, but you must. It is all for Doruf'.

But in fact it was not for Doruf. It was all for Lisie. Dorika wanted to make sure that Lisie would be happy at least a few more days. She wanted her friend's child to feel the goodness of life in the remaining days. Even though she wasn't a believer of relations and sympathy her heart sometimes melted away seeing bizarre circumstances of living beings. The day went on and diminished under the bluish night sky. Dorika and Lisie sung together in the evening. Dorika played the strings of an old *balalaika* melodiously. She sang about a war that took place further back in the history of Serbia. It was about the war between Ottomans and Serbia in the battle fields of Kosovo. Nick heard them singing in Serbian, he could understand from the rhythm that it was a folk song.

Nebo je plavo, Nebo je plavo
Ali Kosovo je crvena.
Lazar je naš junak , On je naše Sunce.
Gledam u nebo , prolazeci vremena, Vidim Lazar'

The *balalaika* flavoured the song with a special melancholic rhythm and longing for the past. In the middle of the song Lisie tried to translate it for Nick. She even tried to recite it in the same tune of Dorika's balalaika strings. She sang,

'The sky is blue, the sky is blue-
But Kosovo is red.
Lazar is our hero, he was our sun.
I looked at the sky, passing time,
I see Lazar'.

It was not the only one they sang. They sang together many other songs too. It seemed to Nick's foreign ears that they were all some folk songs. Some of them were full of energy some others were slow and melancholic. There were songs similar to the monsoon rain with irregular shifts from one tune to other, yet beautiful like all others. It didn't matter to Dorika as she proved even at her old age her fingers were familiar with the balalaika. They didn't let Nick to be silent; they made him sing three or more English songs he knew. He didn't really know much. Music was always Andria's area;

Nick was into reading and sports. Songs about the Serbian country sides and lives of its farmers were sung. After each song Lisie told him a story behind every one of them. The song of Prince Lazar of Serbia who fought bravely the battle of Kosovo and against the mighty Ottomans in 1389 touched Nick's heart when he heard from them that he gave up his life in the battle of Kosovo. Prince Lazar didn't spare the Ottoman Sultan Murad to rule his land. Prince Lazar was truly a legend in the history of Serbia. After hearing the heroic accounts of Prince Lazar those melancholic folk songs carried Nick's mind away from Dorika and Lisie. His mind wandered around the thoughts of similar legendary lives, he thought about William Wallace who fought against England. He asked himself silently,

'How many legends are forgotten in the world? They might have got an unmarked grave in return of their great life.'

When such thoughts began to sadden him deeply, he consoled himself reminding a truth about all legends. He told himself,

'They wouldn't worry. They didn't live to become legends. They didn't want to be remembered. They did everything just to be themselves'.

Dorika insisted them to sleep early. She knew they had a long way to ride in the morning. She knew a long horse ride without enough sleep would demolish both of them. She had a different plan about their journey. But she didn't tell anything about it to Lisie or Nick. Perhaps she wanted to make everything easier for them. They had their supper

158

together. Nick and Dorika hid from Lisie that it was their last supper together. They all slept in the hope of a pleasant morning.

Welcome notes for a new life

Nick and Lisie would have been enjoying some sweet dreams in their sleep while Dorika knocked their door. It was the unique moment in the morning to witness the sun rising behind the mountain ranges of Niš. It didn't take long for them to prepare themselves for the journey. They had the same plans of journey; they thought they would travel as far to the tavern where they spent their night on their way to Avala. They had no idea about the change Dorika was about to make in their ride preparations. They told Dorika about their plan to cover the great distance between Melenci and Avala at one stretch. Dorika wasn't against their plan but she told them about a slight change she wanted them to make in their ride. She told them,

'On your way to Belgrade, you will pass Lužane. It is an old village. You will see a church in Lužane on the left side of the road. The priest would be waiting for you after the morning prayers. I went to see him yesterday, don't you remember? That's why I left you alone here. I have a letter for him. Hand over it and accept whatever he gives you. From there you can continue your journey as you wish'.

They didn't mind to carry a letter to a priest on their way home. They had to pass through Lužane, so they didn't even have to spend any time for that. Dorika was pleased as they were willing to carry her letter. But either Nick or Lisie didn't know the message they carried along with them, in fact they were not even eager to know about it. Kaiser was ready, the sun light made enough room over the narrow roads among the woods and they told good bye to Dorika. Her eyes felt the heat of tears. She knew she would never see Lisie again in her lifetime. She knew she would never see Doruf again or hear about Nick. She kissed them both and wished them a safe journey home. She had to tell a few words to Nick,

'Good luck with your life Nick. I must say you are lucky to have a lovely wife like Andria. You will be freed from Doruf's life. You will wake up in your time like from a dream'. She kept looking at his face with a smile and told him her last words to him,

'Lucky young man, you are special. Good bye'.

'Dorika, I hope to see you soon', Lisie told.

Dorika didn't say anything but kept an innocent smile on her face. She waved her hands as Kaiser slowly started to move. They travelled through the mountain roads. It was easier for Kaiser as they were going down the hill. The mountain wind still blew among the woods but not as strong as in the nights. Black pines danced in the wind as if they were waving at Lisie and Nick. When the sunlight began to be warmer and the remaining mist vanished in the air they were passing across the fields in Lužane village. Lisie told Nick that they were passing through the village Dorika wanted them to meet the priest. Their eyes were looking at both sides for the sight of a church. But they didn't see one until they passed the barren fields of the village. They began to see some households before their eyes and among them they could see a tall building with a cross over its dome. They were sure that it was a church. But they were not sure whether it was the one Dorika mentioned. They had no choice but to walk into the church. They stopped by the church leaving Kaiser alongside the road. A priest in his holy robe was sitting alone inside the church reading something. Lisie took the letter out of her leather bag and approached him. Nick followed her, he was checking how different the robe seemed from the robes used in English churches in the twentieth century. He told in his mind that changes occur even in the case of holy robes.

'Father, bless us', Lisie addressed him in Serbian.

'Peace is upon you, child'. He looked above from his book with a smile. Lisie continued to speak in Serbian. She handed over Dorika's letter. But before that she made it clear that they were at the right place.

'Father, I have a letter from Niš. Do you know Dorika'?

'Yes I know her. We spoke about you last day. If I am not wrong, you are Lisie'.

Lisie didn't know Dorika had a talk with the priest about her. She was left in bewilderment as the priest started reading the letter. It was written in the letter,

'*Bless Father,*

This is Lisie and with her is the man I told you about. His name is Nick. Out of compassion and love for my child Lisie I repeat my request. Please get them married to each other before the Lord. It is the only help we can do for Lisie. Nothing to worry about the man, he knows everything. Please keep everything secret from Lisie. Lisie calls him Doruf so please use 'Doruf' as the man's name in the marriage. Please pronounce them man and wife with your command.

Kissing your right hand'

Dorika'

But unaware of any of these Lisie stood silently beside Nick until the priest finished reading. He gently raised his face towards both of them and asked Lisie,

'Does he speak Serbian? Dorika told me that he can't'.

'He can't father. He speaks only English'. Even while replying him she wasn't sure why Dorika told everything to a priest. She began to wonder what was written in the letter. She didn't ask him anything. But the priest told Nick in English.

162

'So, you are Doruf and Nick together'.

Nick didn't know what to tell. He wasn't expecting it from the priest. But he told him that he was in fact both Doruf and Nick.

'Are you both engaged'?

'Yes', Lisie told him. She even assured him in her next sentence,

'We are'.

The clergyman told them about Dorika's request. He told them that he was ready to get them married in the church under the customary Christian way. He asked them whether they were both ready to get married. It was unexpected for them, even for Lisie. But she didn't think a lot. She was always ready to marry Doruf. She said 'Yes'. But it wasn't sure whether Nick would give the same reply. The priest asked him about it once again as he remained confused. But he said he would marry Lisie. They married each other in the village of Lužane in an empty church. No man witnessed their marriage except the priest. Perhaps some doves and the idol of Christ witnessed their marriage and vow to each other. But as if to be heard to the world, their vow echoed in the empty church like a chant.

The priest announced it before the God,

'Therefore, with the blessings of God, it is my pleasure to now pronounce you husband and wife'.

163

It was over. They kissed each other sealing their marriage vow. It didn't matter how many people attended a marriage or how beautiful they looked, it was all about joining two hearts together forever. If that was the measurement of marriage it definitely was a perfect marriage.

From that moment on they weren't lovers but man and wife. Lisie was sure her father wouldn't be happy with her decision. But she had no other choice. With the blessings of the priest they walked out of the door. Lisie lost herself in the church as she could feel a new individual within her. She became a new person with more responsibilities all of a sudden.

Belgrade was still far away from them. As Kaiser galloped Nick embraced her from behind. They travelled together leaving behind their fears. The distance between each other slowly vanished as they vowed each other as husband and wife. Nick enjoyed the country air that carried the smell of grains and mustard flowers. But Lisie's hair that touched his face in the wind seemed more fragrant to his sense. They travelled almost all day finally reaching Vilko's humble tea shop along the Sava River. They talked with him for some time. He became happy hearing about their marriage and how Dorika helped Nick to realise himself as Doruf. Vilko became talkative about Lisie's mother. He told them how naughty Dijana was at her younger days. He told them how she began to be very serious about practicing witchcraft with them and about the day they all had to leave their own village. Vilko told them how he spent the rest of his life after he left his village. He told them about a young girl whom he loved at his youth. He kept talking,

'She was Zora. We loved each other for around four years even when we were not aware about the depth of love. All I wanted was to live with her. She knew about my secrets that I used to practice witchery with Dorika and your mother. She always tried to stop me from doing that. But she didn't really mind. She often visited me and I used to make tea for her. Our days were nice until one day when her parents found out that I practice witchery. They stopped her from seeing me. But I went to see her at her house in the nights. One night, they found out that we were seeing each other. I ran away from there, I ran away with the hope that I would meet her somehow on the next day'.

Lisie and Nick listened to his past as he continued. But they were left deeply saddened to hear that he never saw her again. He told them he tried to sneak into her house. But never saw her. After a week he came to know that she was taken to her uncle's place somewhere in the south. He told them that he travelled to see her at her uncle's place. But they had sent her to Rome. After some months he was told by some of his friends in Rome that she married a wealthy merchant. That was the point in his life where he gave up witchcraft. He told them both how much he missed Zora even after five decades. He liked making tea for her. So he began to make tea. He made tea for others all his life wandering all over the country. With his savings he went to different places. He travelled far out to the east to see the deserts in Persia. He went to the north until he couldn't travel any longer in the heavy snow. South showed him wildlife and manmade wonders of Egypt. But he returned to the soil of Serbia and made tea for others. He was obsessed with its steam and smell. He stopped his story saying this,

'I always think that I shouldn't have run away. I have travelled to many places just to see the world. The new sights comforted me. But in my entire life I never dared to visit Rome after that. It is just because I am afraid to see one single face'.

They didn't tell him anything. After hearing his story they didn't even wanted to remind him anything of Zora. But Vilko told them a sentence that he told them when he first met them on their way to Avala. He told them that it is hard to remember everything as he grew old. But his youthful memories were haunting him as they were deeply imprinted into his mind. Lisie and Nick were offered a cup of tea before they left him with his own way of life. For some reason both of them felt that they weren't drinking just some tea. They smelt love in the steam that slowly flew up from their cups. Neither Nick nor Lisie ever tasted anything similar to that cup of tea. He didn't take any money for the tea he gave them. That made Lisie relieved because she knew the weight of coins wouldn't be enough to pay its price. The old man waved at them till they finally disappeared from his vision.

They had to spend the night somewhere. They chose the same tavern they used when they were heading to Avala to meet Dorika. But unlike the other night the tavern was silent and almost empty. There were no wandering musicians playing their melodious country songs. They had already left to some other place like migratory birds. Lisie and Nick slept together. They shared their love for each other and the warmth of their body in the night of an unusually rough wind. They could hear the branches of a tiny maple tree grooming on the windows. But nothing stopped them from loving each other.

The night went away while they relaxed in each other's arms. And their travel continued along the Serbian plateau in the morning until they reached Belgrade by the afternoon. They wanted to see Lisie's parents and sisters before they could go to Doruf's house. They had to tell them that they married each other in a church with the authority and presence of a priest. For a village like theirs, especially at their time it was not an act that would easily be accepted. Lisie was well aware of it. Finally when Kaiser stepped into the yard of Lisie's house she told Nick that she was about to tell everything to her father. Kaiser stopped at the door marking an end to their weary ride with a loud and long hiss.

Back in Belgrade

Lisie and Nick were welcomed warmly by her sisters. They were very happy to have them back. Having finished his work in the farm Lisie's father Radmilo was already home. His eyes checked Doruf right away even before he looked at her daughter. Veronica's words that 'Doruf became mad' echoed in his ears. Nick understood that Lisie's father was scrutinising him with his sharp eyes. Nick smiled at him as it was the only polite message he knew to exchange with him without knowing any Serbian. Radmilo was pleased to see him smile as it reduced his unnecessary fear about Doruf. Smile always helps to reduce the unnecessary apprehensions between individuals. Sometimes it is just the absence of a smile that complicates issues among men.

Radmilo looked at her daughter. He could see the trails of a tiring ride all over her. She looked tired and partially consumed by the elements of weather. He asked her sister Lousie to get something for Lisie and Doruf to drink. But Lisie wasn't bothered about her tiredness. She was thinking how to expose her father to certain realities about her life. She wanted to tell him that she was married. She knew he would get heated for doing it in his absence especially when he had everything arranged for them in the August. Then she wanted to tell him about Doruf, who lost all his memory. And that would definitely make him think twice whether he should allow his daughter to marry Doruf. But either of them didn't matter at that point as they were already married. He asked Lisie,

'How was the journey? Did you meet Dorika'?

She told him that they were lucky to meet her. She told him that they were treated very well at her place.

'You look extremely tired, Lisie'. He couldn't hide it from his daughter.

'Yes Papa, I am actually tired. It was hot all day'.

As Lousie brought them some sweetened raspberry juice to

drink Lisie told her father about her marriage. She told him,

'Papa, I married him'.

'Lisie, what did you say'?

'Yes Papa, I married him at Lužane. We were told to get married there. Dorika told us that it was the right time'.

'Could you not have waited for another one month Lisie? What about the date I fixed? What about our people who were waiting for your marriage? What about your sisters and me'?

'Papa, it was necessary'.

The argumentative tone of her father told Nick what was going on. He could imagine that she opened up the news of her marriage. Even though he understood not even one word that was exchanged between Lisie and her father, he remained patient and silent as if he understood everything that was told. Her father couldn't accept her as she expected. He questioned her again and again.

'Lisie, why? Just tell me why? What was the necessity? Just tell me one acceptable excuse'.

'Papa, I can tell you. Please don't get angry, please listen what happened to us'.

Trying to hide his anger from her, he sat on the couch near them. He showed her with his hand to carry on with her explanation. He looked at Doruf without any idea that he was standing there with the identity of another person from another century. Lisie told him what happened to Doruf on the night when there was an unexpected snowfall over Serbian lands even though it was summer. He was slowly exposed to the reality that his daughter's husband had no memory about himself or his parents or even his country. With each word Lisie told him, he was convinced to the comments made by Veronica.

'Doruf is mad, don't let him marry Lisie', those words of Vernica proved to be right in the eyes of Radmilo. But he was agitated with the fact that he was actually helpless to rescue his daughter. Doruf was already Lisie's husband. Their marriage was done before the eyes of the Lord in accordance to the Christian customs and sealed with the marriage vow. There was nothing about it that he could do.

Lisie's sisters smiled at her. They were happy about their sister's marriage. Perhaps only women understood another woman's feelings in achieving everything what they consider precious. In Lisie's case it was Doruf.

Lisie's father couldn't believe it that Doruf forgot himself and even their language. He didn't want to believe in the identity of Nick. So he just thought that it was a mental disorder with Doruf's mind. But he was helpless as Lisie repeated it to him that he wasn't mentally sick but spiritually blessed to have travelled into a century ahead of them. She didn't want to confuse her poor father saying everything Dorika explained to them. She had another plan to make him believe the reality. As her father knew how to speak English, she wanted him to communicate with Doruf. It was Radmilo who taught Lisie how to speak English. He knew how poor

Doruf was with his language skills in English. In fact Doruf used to hate English language for some reason. She asked him to speak with him in English. Radmilo had only one choice, he had to do it. They spoke each other. Just by hearing the way Doruf spoke to him in the typical English accent made him believe that something wasn't Doruf in him. Doruf assured Radmilo with one promise that he wouldn't hurt his daughter. He told him,

'I don't really know how to make you believe my words. It's true I am not able to remember any of you, but still I love Lisie. She is my wife now'.

Radmilo heard everything Nick told him. He felt like he was listening to a fairy tale, yet undeniably real.

'Did you tell this to his parents, Lisie'?

'No Papa. But we are going to tell it'.

He advised them to tell it gently. Because for them, it wasn't about a marriage but it was about their own son. To them it meant their son forgot everything, including themselves. He was sure they wouldn't handle it easily. He didn't want Lisie to stay there any longer because she was in fact supposed to be at her husband's house. Although they couldn't be at her wedding they hugged her and kissed her before they sent her with Doruf to his house. Even if they were going to Doruf's house, it was obvious he didn't know his own house or the way that lead to it. In fact he was sent with Lisie to his own house as a loyal husband.

Radmilo asked Lisie to take Kaiser along with her, because

he knew Kaiser wouldn't like to be there without Lisie. As Lisie and Kaiser walked along their village road her sisters told her aloud that they would visit her at Doruf's house in the evening. Lisie was fondling Kaiser and they could see from the yard that she was even talking with him. They went back into their house quickly to get ready to visit their newly married sister.

It was nothing different when they reached Doruf's house. Doruf's mother and father had been eagerly waiting for their return. When they saw their son they wanted to make it clear that he completely recovered from his illness. They were actually worried about him a lot. They were told that he went to Niš with Lisie for a medical observation. That was how Lisie took him from his parents. Doruf didn't answer to any of their questions but smiled gently to show them that he was all right. Lisie tried to answer every question when Nick remained silent. She took some time to finally tell his parent's what happened to him. She told it very calmly to his father,

'I need to tell you something about Doruf. There is nothing to be worried'.

'What happened, Lisie'?

She told him that Doruf didn't get his memory back. She told them about the strange condition Doruf underwent and his vision into his own future. As Lisie kept explaining to his parents what happened to him, his mother started crying. But Lisie continued,

'It's nothing wrong with his mind. It is actually his speciality

173

that made him able to see his future. In his eyes, we are all part of a world that has become past in his time. He says he is Nick from England. He lives there with his wife Andria and to him his present year is 2014. We, as we are living in 1914 is a past time for him'.

'Lisie, this is all nonsense. He needs proper medication and care. What did the doctor say'?

His mother couldn't hide her disagreement. It was normal from an ordinary person to have the similar kind of reaction. Like others she was also pointing indirectly that he was mentally weak. But Lisie wasn't ready to give up. She told her,

'No, he is not sick. Even I thought it was his illness in the beginning. But I gave him a chance to prove himself right. If he was mentally weak, how can he forget our language and talk another foreign language fluently? He never spoke in English, but he knows only English at the moment. He doesn't even remember our language. He doesn't remember me or even you. But he knows that he is trapped in his own past. He knows Doruf is as real as him. He is ready to live among us, we have to believe him. We have to give him a chance to prove everything'.

Lisie told them about Dorika and what she informed them about Nick and all other lives he had. Doruf's mother asked him whether he could remember her. But Nick didn't understand her. She told her in return,

'Mother, I don't understand Serbian. But I know what you

are asking. I don't remember you, but I know you are my mother'.

Lisie had to translate his sentence for his mother. She broke into tears hearing what her son wanted to tell her. Lisie knew she should tell her about their marriage. She thought it would make them happy to realise that she wasn't ready to give up Doruf. She always called Doruf's mother 'Mama' and his father 'Tata'. She addressed them before telling them about their marriage,

'Mama, Tata, I want to tell something else'.

As they curiously looked at her she continued,

'We are married. We married in the church of Lužane. I know I should have waited till the August, but Dorika told us that it would be helpful for Doruf's recovery if we married earlier. She arranged our marriage there, so we did it'.

Lisie was correct, they were really happy to hear the news. It wasn't the marriage that made them glad but the realisation that Lisie didn't let him down even at a challenging point of his life. They were glad that their son was lucky to have Lisie in his life. She definitely was a very nice person to spend a whole life together. Lisie's confidence definitely helped his parents to believe everything would be all right in the near future. Lisie informed his mother that her sisters would visit them in the evening. They both engaged themselves preparing a delicious dinner for her sisters as it was in fact a wedding feast. They arrived to see their sister and her husband before the sunset. They spent the evening together

175

celebrating the wedding modestly. The news spread across their village that Lisie and Doruf married at Lužane. Their friends went over to their house to see the newly married couple. All of them were exposed to the reality that Doruf had lost his memory. But no one bothered about it as he behaved politely how he used to do when he had his memory. He didn't understand most of their questions and comments but language failed to diminish the grace of that wonderful evening. Lisie helped him a lot by translating everything he wanted to say. Slowly he became familiar to most of the villagers. In other words, he slowly found himself again.

But Veronica wasn't happy to hear about their wedding. She had planned everything perfectly to abort their marriage. She even inflicted her venom successfully in Lisie's father to make him believe that Doruf was out of his mind. If Lisie and Doruf came back without marrying each other, her plan would have been successful. Because after hearing everything from Lisie, her father didn't want her daughter to marry Doruf. Perhaps Dorika was aware of Veronica's intention with her supernatural senses. That could be the reason why she wanted them to get married as early as they could. She made everything a lot easier for Lisie and Doruf indeed. Veronica didn't attend their wedding feast. Lisie was fortunate to get away from Veronica's vengeance. Sometimes even without our knowledge we might be being helped even from the farthest distances like Dorika helped Lisie from Veronica's snare.

The evening went away spreading grace over the life they just began. The guests were all gone even Lisie's sisters and parents. But the house remained cherished with the four human beings in it, Lisie, Doruf and his parents. They just started a new life out of the scraps they collected with their long tiring journey. They slept peacefully and woke up to a new month, the month of July 1914.

Lisie stopped working in the mustard farms and started to work with Nick in the cornfields. They took care of the plants together. Nick didn't know much about farming but it was his favourite when he used to be Doruf. Lisie taught him how to nurture the plants and to spot the weeds growing among the corn seedlings. With her assistance he slowly began to be interested in farming. He woke up early before Lisie and walked through the cornfields. Within a few days he learnt to take care of a cornfield without Lisie. Sometimes Lisie found him sitting in the cornfields all by himself. One day she asked him what was in his mind. He told her,

'Nothing else Lisie, I am thinking about myself. I am thinking how I slowly change and adapt to this way of life. I like being in the fields caring these plants, breathing this air that has the smell of soaked soil and dry leaves. I have started loving you. I am wondering how I don't even realise that I was called Nick'.

He was right. He changed a lot with those few days. Even Lisie noticed how he changed himself while adapting to Doruf's world. But as days passed by Nick's fear grew stronger about the approaching day of destruction. He wanted to tell Lisie that they should run away from there to escape from the ferocious attacks. But he was also reminded of Dorika's words that 'destiny would follow them, no matter how far the try to run away'. So he didn't tell anything about it to Lisie. He waited for the day like a condemned man in a cell. He waited for it; he knew he would have to walk to the gallows in the coming days.

Every evening after their work in the farms they walked along the country roads until the moon shined bright above the cornfields. They sat near Sava River almost every evening if the weather was good. It was there they discussed about everything. Nick asked her about the political problems in Europe. She told them everything she knew from the news papers. He didn't have any hope that the world war would spare their life. And from Lisie he came to know that the German Empire was also ready to support Austrians if they want a war against Serbia. There was also a rumour in the news papers that the Russian Empire would support Serbia in case of an emergency as France already talked about it with the Russia. Nick could clearly see from that news what was about to happen in a couple of days. He reminded himself the dates of the month as it was already 19th of July 1914. Only Nick knew how deadly that war was about to be. Even the rulers of those countries perhaps didn't know how long it was going to be or how many men were about be slaughtered in the coming years. The days went away one after one and Nick's heart was absolutely ready for it when the day light of 27th of July diminished. He knew the day was going to break with the violent war savaging the villages and its people. He couldn't sleep that night because he didn't know whether the war would hit them while they sleep. He didn't let Lisie know that he couldn't get any sleep. He walked in the room sleepless and troubled. His heart pounded, he was sweating all night even though the night remained a little colder. But Lisie woke up very early in the morning around three o'clock and saw him walking inside the room. She knew something was wrong with Doruf. She found out that he was stressed about something. She tried to calm him down and tried to get him some sleep. But when she laid her head on his chest trying to comfort, she could hear his heart beating dangerously faster. He didn't tell her what bothered him so much. He kept saying he saw a nighmare. But finally Lisie's love and embraces calmed him down. He got some sleep for around three hours.

Nick woke up into the daylight. He checked whether he was alive there, he checked whether everything looked similar, he even checked for Lisie. He found her in the kitchen. Seeing him awake she asked him,

'How do you feel now?'

Her question made it clear that he was still alive there. He couldn't believe it that the war didn't break out so far. But he knew that there was plenty of time still to go in the day. He replied her,

'I am okay. But, I don't want to go to work'.

'Why, are you feeling sick'?

'I think so. Just want to rest'.

But in fact he was afraid to go out. He didn't even let Lisie to go out to the cornfields. The day looked calm and quite like all other wonderful days. The wind blew from the west fondling the thick and dry corn leaves. The sky was as clear as a blue piece of cloth.

Nick finally strengthened himself by the afternoon. He could see no hints about the war. But there were rumours that the Austrians might attack them. As it was an everyday news for the last few weeks nobody was worried about it that much. Most of them were busy with their work in the cornfields and mustard farms except Lisie and Nick. Finally by the evening, Nick and Lisie went out for their daily walk. He still hid from her why he didn't go out of the house for the whole day. They walked up to the Sava River and sat there for some time. His fear was all in vain, there was no clue of any kind of attack. They talked about their work for tomorrow. She told him about cleaning the weed in their cornfield and about her plans to start mustard farming in the next season.

Sava River was pleasant in the twilight. There were some boats moving along the river. It was a beautiful sight. Nick looked at them as they approached slowly. But suddenly he noticed its unusual appearance. They all had bright lights attached to their rear and sides, there was a very long antenna in the middle of those big size boats. As their engines began to be more audible to Nick, he jumped up holding her hand. He hid behind the trees with Lisie. She didn't understand what happened to him. But he asked her to be very silent, his hands were trembling. He heard its sound approaching, its sound echoed in the woods. He peeped from behind the trees to check their movement. He was shocked when he saw those boats getting closer to their shore. They weren't small, they were larger than they seemed from a distance. Lisie asked him very silent,

'Who are they'? She was also terrified with the sound of those giant engines.

'Lisie', He stopped his words in confusion whether he should say it to her or not. But his tongue slipped, he said,

'They are battle ships. Don't even move'.

But they were late. They were spotted by the guards of the ship. It was just a matter of getting them in the range of their guns. All of sudden a continuous explosive sound was heard. And they could see the leaves of the trees just a few feet away from them spattered in front of them. Then within a few seconds the sound was heard again but this time the tree which they used as their cover trembled. They saw its wood being torn apart like a piece of paper. Nick cried,

'Lisie, they are firing at us. Run away'.

He didn't even try to hide anywhere as he knew it would be a pointless effort. He ran holding her hand as quickly as he could through the woods. But the bullet fired from mini guns and shells narrowly missed their two moving targets. But it didn't happen for a long time. A few of the bullets fired from a gun did splash out the blood in the veins of Doruf. He cried aloud,

'Lisie..'

He dropped her hand and fell down. Pain from the bullet

was severe. It had destroyed his ribs and lungs. He pressed the left side of his chest while calling out her name. It didn't take too long for his creamy white shirt to turn red. Lisie was almost fainting seeing his blood dripping on the dried leaves. He managed to say one last word,

'Run'.

But Lisie didn't, she sat down holding his hands and his blood spread on her skirt even before she held his head to her lap. His voice was inaudible but the look in his eyes told her to run for her life. Tears flowed from her eyes and dripped one by one on his wound melting in his blood.

'Don't leave me, Dorf. I am scared, I am scared. Don't leave me alone Dorf, don't'.

Doruf wasn't able to say a word, he was out of breath. The advancing armed men surrounded Lisie on their gun points. Lisie uttered one last sentence before they dragged her from him,

'Dorf, I want to live with you. Don't leave me alone'

'I can't lose you Lisie, I want to live',

He was trying to say that but his lungs had no air left. At that point he couldn't remember that he was Nick. He felt the pain of Doruf's wounds and he spat out Doruf's blood. He wanted to save her from them but he was losing his vision and he was failing to inhale. He tried hard to breath in the air around him, but his lungs couldn't hold it inside.

Those were the last words he heard from Lisie. He didn't hear anything else thereafter as his ears failed to hear. He didn't feel his pain for a moment as if he wasn't aware of his body. He saw them dragging her out of his sight. That was the last sight he saw before an absolute darkness rushed into his eyes. He died there if that is the right word but Lisie was just forgotten, no one ever told what happened to her.

Awakening

'Lisie...' he called her name aloud. As if he was recalling everything he began to utter in a fainted voice.

'I am lost...help me Lisie...Lisie... Yes, yes I love Andria. I don't know your language. No, I don't belong here...cornfields. This is Serbia. Vilko...Dorika...'

He went on describing the scenes in his eyes. Some people say just a moment before our life ends each single scene from the very childhood days to the last scene would flash with the speed of light in our mind. Perhaps that was happening in his case.

'Lisie run away. Please don't harm her. I can't breathe...I can't breathe...I can't see anything...I am dying. Lisie'.

He tried to get out of its grip. It was hard; it was very hard to get out of that emptiness. There was nothing else but an absolute darkness around him. It wasn't because he couldn't see anything, but it was black in colour. He could see it with his very own eyes. He wanted to cry for some help. But there was no one there to seek help. There was no point as well because he could feel he wasn't trapped in it, he was just being a part of it. He told himself to calm down. He tried to touch his body, but he couldn't touch it. He had no physical features, he was the black element which surrounded him, he was empty. He asked himself,

'Where am I, what have I become'?

There was a sound, he heard it very closely. It was a very light sound. It sounded like a giant wave passing through a tunnel from one end to the other. It began as a loud noise and feebly vanished somewhere away. It repeated for some time in a regular interval. Then gently he was awakening, lights began to show up from somewhere into his eyes. He could hear the sound of an electronic device beeping beside him. He was able to see everything; it was a very clean room. He could feel his body and he saw a woman passing by him. She wasn't bothered about him as she was writing something on a long white paper. He slowly understood that he was in a hospital room and the woman in front of him was perhaps a nurse or a doctor. He wanted to call her.

'Hi', his voice was thin. But she heard him. He didn't understand why she became so happy when he called her. She rushed towards him with a curious smile. She asked him,

'Hi, how are you'?

'I'm just fine, where is Lisie. Is she okay'?

The lady was confused about the name Lisie. She asked him as she wanted to make it clear,

'Is that your wife's name'?

'Yes, she's my wife. Who took me here'?

The nurse had no idea about the name of his wife. She told him,

'She is right here, I will call her. Don't you want to see her'?

185

'Yeah, please call her'. Nick told her with his weak voice and eagerly waited to see Lisie. But it wasn't Lisie who came to meet him. It was his wife Andria who came with tears on her face. She grabbed his hands and cried for some time. Nick was happy to see her beside him. He has been waiting to see her face from the day he was trapped in Serbia. But he looked around the room checking another face too. He asked Andria,

'Ann, where is Lisie'?

Andria didn't know who Lisie was. She looked at his face. He was looking around the room as if he was seriously looking for somebody. Lisie looked around, and asked him,

'Who is Lisie? Is that the nurse'?

'No, Ann. She...my wife. Lisie'.

Andria thought he was still not completely aware of everything. She tried to explain it to him,

'Nick, look at me. I am Ann, your wife. I don't know Lisie. I am your wife'. She smiled at him. But he continued,

'Yes Ann, you are my wife. But I married Lisie in Serbia when I was there'.

Andria wanted to laugh. But she controlled her laughter and asked him when he travelled to Serbia. He told her like an innocent toddler,

'I didn't go there. I was there; I was a Serbian before I met you'.

Andria allowed him to say everything but she didn't believe a single word he uttered. She rejected every truthful detail he told her about some life that was also as truthful as her own life was with a smile. That was exactly what the Serbian villagers did when Doruf told them about Nick. They called him madman for saying a truth that seemed impossible in their eyes. Andria didn't call him a madman, but she believed that he wasn't completely recovered from his sickness. He had been admitted in the hospital for the last two weeks after an internal bleeding occurred in his brain.

Nick cried. He wanted to see Lisie. He wanted to know what happened to her. He loved her so much; he loved her the same way how he loved Andria. He shed his tears for Lisie who lived a century before him. That was the present war brought him after hundred years. He wasn't sure what happened to her. It would have been easier to accept if she was dead. Nick might perhaps live all his life with the memories of a wasteful violence men committed towards each other. He may forget about Lisie when he starts his life with Andria once again. But how sad is it? The reminiscences of the war came to haunt his life even after ten decades.

Andria wanted to console him. But she didn't realise the reality in his surreal statements. It is humane not to believe certain facts just because they never had a chance to experience it. Like the English poet John Keats wrote, *'Nothing ever becomes real till it is experienced'*.

But there is another way you can think about everything. Time and place, both are fictional. Find a lonely tree in the middle of a cornfield and sit beneath its trembling leaves in the solitude of an evening. And ask yourself,

'Do they really exist? Do we really exist'?

***

ॐ पूर्णमदः पूर्णमिदम्
पूर्णात् पूर्णमुदच्यते
पूर्णस्य पूर्णमादाय
पूर्णमेवावशिष्यते
ॐ शान्तिः शान्तिः शान्तिः

ABOUT THE AUTHOR

Vinayaka Moorthi MK , born on April 12, 1992 in Alappuzha, Kerala as first son to Mrs. Beas and Mr. Krishnamoorthy. He was raised in the village of Pallaatthuruth North on the banks of Vembanad lake and River Pampa. After finishing lower school education Vinayak moved to the Cherthala with his family and continued his education till graduation. He moved to Coventry, UK for his post-graduation in the year 2012 and worked in the Republic of Maldives as a college lecturer. Later he continued teaching in India along with his own tastes of education. His first novel was published in the year 2014 in the UK titled 'I Met A Fairy Queen'. Apart from writing he concentrates on teaching English and learning linguistics.